Please return/renew this item by the last date shown. Books may also be renewed by phone or internet.

💻 www3.rbwm.gov.uk/libraries

☎ 01628 796969 (library hours)

☎ 0303 123 0035 (24 hours)

www.rbwm.gov.uk

Royal Borough
of Windsor &
Maidenhead

Praise for *Land of Big Numbers*

'Gripping and illuminating, *Land of Big Numbers* offers intimate glimpses of the seductive power of state control: the Faustian bargaining it requires of its citizens, the landscapes and lives it forces them to discard in exchange for material prosperity. At the heart of Te-Ping Chen's remarkable debut lies a question all too relevant in twenty-first Century America: What is freedom?'
—Jennifer Egan, Pulitzer Prize-winning author of *A Visit from the Goon Squad* and *Manhattan Beach*

'Immensely rewarding, from the first sentence to the last. Te-Ping Chen's writing is clear-eyed, pitch perfect, skilfully restrained and quietly powerful. I will be returning to these stories again, to enjoy them, be consoled by them, and marvel at them. An exceptional collection.'
—Charles Yu, author of the National Book Award finalist *Interior Chinatown*

'Te-Ping Chen's *Land of Big Numbers* is ripe with prose both sharp and beautiful. There is a rare brilliance and a feeling of necessity imbued in every word of these stories. At each story's end you feel wonderfully more awake, more connected and alive. This essential collection reminds us clearly that there is magic and violence all around us. This is a stunning debut.'
—Nana Kwame Adjei-Brenyah, *New York Times* bestselling author of *Friday Black*

'An intricately constructed, tenderly observed collection—the sort of stories that skillfully transport you into the daily experience of characters so real, who speak to you with such grace and tangible presence, that you could almost reach out and touch them.

Through the lens of these different voices, each vividly alive, Te-Ping Chen shows us how much life, loss, and quiet pleasure exists in the world, just out of view.'
—Alexandra Kleeman, author of *You Too Can Have a Body Like Mine* and *Intimations*

'This debut story collection is absolute fire. It has the great quixotic feel of being both ancient and modern all at once. I think fans of Megha Majumdar, Kamila Shamsie, and Jhumpa Lahiri would love this one!'—Amy Jo Burns, author of *Shiner*

'A spectacular work, comic, timely, profound. Te-Ping Chen has a superb eye for detail in a China where transformation occurs simultaneously too fast and too slow for lives in pursuit of meaning in a brave new world. Her characters are achingly alive. It's rare to read a collection so satisfying, where every story adds to a gripping and intricate world.'
—Madeleine Thien, author of Booker finalist *Do Not Say We Have Nothing*

'A book brimming with quietly devastating stories about Chinese men and women wrestling with the notion of home.'
—*O, the Oprah Magazine*

'The often haunting stories in Chen's strong debut follow characters striving for better futures in China as buried memories begin to surface ... Chen's sweeping collection comprises many small moments of beauty.'—*Publishers Weekly*

'Subtle, haunting, beautiful short stories of life in an unfree society.'
—Steve Inskeep of NPR's Morning Edition, via Twitter

LAND OF BIG NUMBERS

LAND OF BIG NUMBERS

TE-PING CHEN

SCRIBNER

LONDON NEW YORK SYDNEY TORONTO NEW DELHI

First published in the United States by Houghton Mifflin Harcourt, 2021
First published in Great Britain by Scribner, an imprint of
Simon & Schuster UK Ltd, 2021

SCRIBNER and design are registered trademarks of The Gale Group, Inc.,
used under licence by Simon & Schuster Inc.

1 3 5 7 9 10 8 6 4 2

Simon & Schuster UK Ltd
1st Floor
222 Gray's Inn Road
London WC1X 8HB

www.simonandschuster.co.uk
www.simonandschuster.com.au
www.simonandschuster.co.in

Simon & Schuster Australia, Sydney
Simon & Schuster India, New Delhi

A CIP catalogue record for this book is available from the British Library

Hardback ISBN: 978-1-4711-9059-9
Trade Paperback ISBN: 978-1-3985-0336-6
eBook ISBN: 978-1-4711-9060-5

Book design by Mark R. Robinson
Printed in the UK by CPI Group (UK) Ltd, Croydon, CR0 4YY

To my parents

CONTENTS

LAND OF BIG NUMBERS

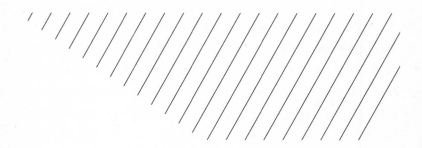

LULU

THE HOUR OF OUR BIRTH HAD BEEN CAREFULLY FORECAST, A WINTER'S DAY CESAREAN TIMED TO COINCIDE WITH DR. FENG'S LUNCH BREAK. The doctor pulled me out first, indignant, squalling, like a hotel guest inexpertly roused and tossed before checkout. She came next, and was so perfectly quiet that at first they worried she wasn't breathing at all. Then they thwacked her on the back and her cries joined mine and they laid us side by side, boy and girl, two underwater creatures suddenly forced to fill our lungs with cold, dry air.

Dr. Feng had operated on my mother as a favor to my uncle, his old classmate. Otherwise we would have been born in the hospital down the street, where a woman had bled to death after a botched cesarean the previous year. The family had been in the waiting room for hours, and at last the father-to-be pounded on the doors of the operating room. When no one responded, the family pushed them open to find the lifeless woman on the table, blood pooling on the ground. She was alone: the staff had stripped the medical certificates that bore their names from the wall and fled as soon as the surgery went wrong.

From the start we were lucky, not least because we had each other. As twins we'd been spared the reach of the government's family-planning policies, two winking fetuses floating in utero. For the first few weeks of our life, our skulls had matching indentations from where they'd been pressed against each other in the womb, like two interlocking puzzle pieces. Later in life when we were apart, I'd sometimes touch my hand to the back of my skull when I thought of her, as if seeking a phantom limb.

We weren't in any way an extraordinary family. My mother worked as a warehouse clerk, my father a government sanitation planner. When my father was forty-seven, his division chief—a fanciful man who had once dreamed of being an artist—decided to build a public toilet in the shape of a European clock tower. He'd been to Europe and had been impressed by the cleanliness of the toilets and the loveliness of the architecture and wanted to combine the two. Like most artists, the division chief had a fragile ego, and shortly after my father balked at the project's expense, he was fired. It was the sole act of independence he'd committed in his life, and it cost him his career.

The toilet still stands there today, its vaulting concrete walls stained and ridiculous, the inside chilly and damp like the inside of a pipe, a bird of poured concrete plunging from the tower's top as if being defenestrated by rival birds inside, and indeed the whole structure smells like a foul aviary. You wouldn't think it cost 200,000 yuan to build, and probably it didn't, Lulu said; most of it likely ended up in the division head's pocket, art corrupting life, life corrupting art.

From the time she was ten, my parents worshipped at Lulu's altar. Her precocity was evident early on; it was like a flag being waved energetically from a mountaintop. Neither of our parents had much education, and it stunned them to find themselves in possession of such a daughter.

When we were small, we played devotedly together. Lulu was a great inventor of games, which often incorporated whatever she'd read most recently: one day we were stinkbugs, looking for the right leaf on which to lay our eggs, another we were herdsmen fleeing Mongolian invaders. She was braver than me: once, when the elderly woman who lived opposite us had left her door ajar while retrieving the mail downstairs, my sister even snuck into her apartment.

"It's full of newspapers, stacked as high as your head," Lulu said excitedly, her eyes glowing as she dashed back. "There's a giant orange cross-stitch on her couch, with a peony and six fishes."

As a child she was always reading. Even at meals she would sit and scan the back of the juice box. She must have read it a million times: aspartame and xanthan gum and red no. 9. It wasn't a conscious thing; she just seemed to feel uncomfortable when her eyes weren't fastened to a page. She had a mania for lists, too. By age eleven she'd memorized every bone in the human body, and she used to recite their names to me at night in an eerie voice as I held a pillow over my head: sternum, tibia, floating rib.

In high school, I rebelled against her brilliance by playing video games, lots of them, spending hours whipping a gun back and forth across dusty landscapes empty of people, except for those who wanted to kill you. Usually there were six or seven of us at my friend Xingjian's apartment, and we would take turns and cheer one another on. We were an army, invincible, or if we weren't invincible we could hit *replay* at any time, which was pretty close to the same thing.

Lulu, meanwhile, was a model among model students. She studied so intensely that it left her physically bowed and exhausted, like an athlete running a daily marathon, and at night she dropped off to sleep without a word. My mother fed her stewed mushrooms that looked like tiny brains when their stems fell off; they would be good for Lulu's studies, she said. She gave me some as well, though by then it was plain that any hopes for academic glory resided with her daughter, not her son, constructive effects of mushrooms be damned.

When we sat for the college entrance exam, it surprised no one that Lulu scored high enough to earn a place at a university in the nation's capital, a bus and a train and a plane ride away. My mother wept with what she said was happiness. "A scholar," she kept saying. "A scholar." She and my father, she liked to remind us, hadn't studied long before going to work in the factories.

"We are so proud," my father told Lulu. There was an intensity to his expression that unnerved me. One of our schoolbooks had a black-and-white illustration of a long-ago eunuch serving a feast, staring hungrily at the food on the emperor's table, and there was something of that look on my father's face.

The night Lulu flew out was overcast, the twilight that preceded it a peculiar mix of orange and ocher. Earlier that day, my father had given her a gift: her very own laptop. It was thick with promise, like a fat slice of cake, sheathed in blue plastic. It wasn't like the old computer that we all shared, which stuttered and stalled, keys sticky with grease and crumbs and bits of hair. This one had keys that yielded obediently when you touched them. I'd stared at it enviously, too filled with longing for words. "Don't worry—you'll get one, too, when you leave, the exact same," my father said.

At the airport, our parents assumed expressions appropriate for refugees being abandoned at a border. "Lulu, be good," our father said. I stood there awkwardly, a little resentfully. Lulu turned and flashed a peace sign as she went through security, and we watched her pink hoodie and striped zebra baseball hat retreat into the crowd until she was gone.

I departed for college a week later, with considerably less fanfare. The school was just an hour's drive away and had an empty feel to it, as though it had been erected with much ambition years ago and then forgotten. In the winter the dorms were freezing, as if their concrete walls held in all the damp, cold air and kept it close to your skin; it looked like a convincing enough building, but felt like a tent.

The best thing about college, I decided, was that the dorms were wired for the internet. There were five other boys in my room on the second floor, sharing rickety metal bunk beds draped with mosquito nets, which afforded both a thin sense of privacy and protection from bites in the summer. At night when we sat in front of our computers, you could hear the same tinny chirping of chat alerts all around us, emanating from the floorboards, the ceilings, and the walls, as though hordes of invisible, electronic crickets had stormed the building.

I wasn't old enough to miss Lulu. Anyway, I could see her chat statuses whenever I logged in on my new laptop, smooth and shiny and housed in a blue plastic sleeve that matched my sister's. *Studying,* they might say. *Going to class.* At some point they got more fanciful. *Floating down the green river,* one read. *Digging into a stone with no edges.* Sometimes I tried looking them up while waiting for my gamer teammates to log on. A few belonged to old poets, but the rest, I suspected, she was inventing herself.

I died repeatedly that semester, but amassed several hundred gold coins and was first made a warlock, then a mage. The other boys in my dorm were addicts, too, and we played fiercely into the evening, cussing, headphones on, until midnight, when the power was cut. Classes were a negligible affair: what mattered were your grades on the final exams, and those could be readily crammed for by memorizing ten or fifteen photocopied pages of notes sold by upperclassmen. Honestly, I had no idea who actually went to class:

I pictured teachers sitting with their laptops in front of empty rooms, one eye on the clock, maybe playing video games of their own, maybe taking a nap.

In our second year of school, I searched idly for one of Lulu's statuses and found just one result: a public microblog with a profile photo of a yawning yellow cat. There were several dozen posts, mostly the same kinds of snippets of poetry Lulu had been posting to her statuses, and by the time I finished scrolling through them, I was sure the account was hers. For the bio she'd written *qiushi,* a reference to the old Communist maxim "to seek truth from facts," but the name of her account was *qiu zhushi,* "to seek carbohydrates," which made me laugh. You wouldn't have suspected it to look at her, but Lulu was a glutton—she could eat reams of noodles or fried crullers without missing a beat.

One day in the dorm, I answered a knock at our door to find a classmate grinning at me. "Your sister's here," he said. I gaped and went downstairs. There she was, wearing an old-fashioned padded blue coat, the kind common in the fifties. Lulu had her hair in two braids, carried a knapsack slung over one shoulder, and was smiling. She'd joined the college debate club, she said, and they were traveling for a competition. "Big Brother," she said—it was an old joke of hers, since I was born only a minute or so before her— "want to buy me dinner?"

I suggested the cafeteria. She said she had something nicer in mind, and took me by the arm to a coffee shop by the campus entrance. The place called itself Pretty O.J.; its sign advertised Italian noodles. I'd walked by dozens of times and never gone in. Inside, the tables were topped with glass and the seats were an uncomfortable white wicker that crackled when you shifted, and there were white vases to match, filled with plastic flowers. Lulu took hold of the menu and confidently ordered a pizza and tomato pasta for us as though she'd done it many times before. "With coffee, please," she added, "and bring us some bread."

I stared at her. "You look happy," I said. She was. She was debating at a college an hour's drive south, she said, and had taken a bus to come to see me. I asked her if our parents knew, if she was planning to see them as well.

"No," she said, smiling. "We fly back tomorrow night, but I wanted to come see you."

Beside her I felt very young in my rubber sandals and T-shirt and shorts. She asked me about my classes and my friends. I told her that I was watching a lot of television on my laptop and playing even more video games. Lately I'd been playing with a team of Russian teenagers who were pretty good. We didn't speak the same language, so we communicated in a kind of pidgin English: *Don't worry guys I got phantom princess no no no, you NOOB, dafuq.*

"I know you think it's a waste of time," I said.

"A lot of kids play it at my school, too," she said, not contradicting me.

"It's a profession now, you know," I said. "They have competitions, you can win big prize money."

It embarrasses me now to realize that up until that point, we'd spent the whole evening talking about my life. I don't think I asked her anything about her own, and it was only at the end that she volunteered a few facts. She was pregnant, she said, two months along, and very much in love with the baby's father.

I choked on the coffee. Lulu waited for me to compose my-self, and then she told me the rest of the story. The father, an up-perclassman studying accounting, was from a poor county in the northeast. No, they weren't keeping the baby, though she and Zhangwei would likely get pregnant again in a few years, "after we're married," Lulu said, with a calm matter-of-factness that as-tounded me. Someday, the two of them hoped to travel abroad.

She told me more about him, choosing her words carefully. "He's not like other people," she said. "He's very noble." It was a strange word, an old-fashioned word. I just stared at her.

"You're sure about all this, Lulu?"

"I'm sure."

I envied her for a moment, sitting there, looking so certain. When had I ever been sure of anything? For Lulu, everything had always come so easily and confidently: homework, answers on tests, college, and now, it seemed, love as well.

When the bill arrived, I didn't have enough money with me, so she paid. "Thanks, Big Brother," she said when we left, and at first I thought she was being sarcastic, but she looked glad when she said it. "I haven't told anyone else," she confessed as we walked out into the blue twilight, the boxy concrete façades of campus around us. "I knew I could trust you."

It was the first time it had occurred to me that I was trustwor-thy, and it was a relief to hear that I had been evaluated and not found wanting. "Of course," I said.

In the following months, I checked her account more often. I got flashes of insight into her life that way: photos of the yellow shocks of forsythia that blossomed in the spring, more odd bits of poetry. I pictured her tapping away at her identical blue-sheathed laptop across the country, clicking *send*.

That fall, she started posting daily about someone named Xu Lei. It was a name that even I'd heard by then, enough people were talking about him. He was a college student who'd been picked up by the police outside a karaoke joint, and been beaten, and died while in custody. Photos of him before his death had circulated online: skinny legs in shorts, glasses, a purple T-shirt that read LET'S GO. He and his friends had been standing outside after singing karaoke, a little drunk, and when police had told them to move along, Xu Lei got caustic and the officers took offense. His friends had filmed them beating him and then loading him into a police van. As quickly as censors took down the footage, it was uploaded again.

Mostly Lulu was just recirculating other people's messages, adding her own hashtag, #justiceforXuLei, or an indignant, frowning face. At some point she added her own commentary: *This country, these police, are simply too dark.*

When the police autopsy came out, it found that Xu Lei had died of a heart attack. The conclusion was promptly met with scorn — he was only eighteen. The coroner's report said that prior to his death, he'd been working hard and not sleeping well. "It was a young person's heart attack," it concluded, a phrase that quickly trended online until censors snuffed it out. Lulu was not impressed. *I have studied hard all my life and I don't sleep well,* she wrote. *Will I, too, be made to have a heart attack?*

After that, Lulu's account became more active. At first she was just reposting news from other accounts: the tainted-formula

scandal that killed three babies, the college admissions adminis-
trator found to be taking cash bribes—the kinds of things we all
knew and groused about.

A few months later, though, she began to flood her account
with images and videos that were genuinely surprising. I had no
idea where she was getting them. They were of scattered street
protests from around the country, some just stills, others clips of
perhaps a few seconds, rarely more than a minute long. *Hubei, Lu-
zhou City, Tianbei County, Mengshan Village: 10 villagers protest outside government offices over death of local woman*, one might say. Or: *Shandong, Cai-
guang City, Taining County, Huaqi Village: 500 workers strike for three days,
protesting over unpaid wages.*

There were dozens of these posts, and they usually looked similar: police in pale blue shirts, lots of shouting, crowds massing in
the streets, occasionally someone on the ground being beaten. In
one video, several men were attempting to tip over a police van.
In another, a group of villagers was shouting as something that
looked horribly like a human figure smoldered on the ground.

They were like dispatches from a country I had never seen, and
they disturbed and confused me.

After seeing the video of the self-immolation, I messaged her.
Are you okay? I asked.

The reply came a few hours later: *Hi, Big Brother! I'm doing fine.*

Are you in Beijing?

Of course I'm in Beijing.

I stared at the blinking cursor. I'd never told her that I knew
her identity online, and I worried that if I said something, she'd see
me as somehow untrustworthy, as though I'd been spying on her.

Beijing must be very cold now, I wrote at last. *Make sure you wear warm clothes.*

That February, we both went home to see our parents and celebrate the Spring Festival. I took charge of the dumplings, chopping the fennel and leeks, cracking an egg and swirling it about with gusto. I was happy. The week before, our team had entered into a local competition and had won a month's supply of instant noodles and certain bragging rights. *Replay, replay:* my fingers knew the commands so instinctively that sometimes I'd wake in the dark with fingers twitching.

Lulu, though, seemed only partly present; often you had to call her name twice to get a response. Sometimes I'd get up to use the bathroom in the middle of the night and see a glow in the living room, which meant she was awake, and online.

One night we gathered around the television watching the Spring Festival gala. It was an annual tradition put on by the state broadcaster: cheesy skits, patriotic odes, terrible slapstick—the whole country watched. I excused myself and logged on to check Lulu's account. The most recent post was from that evening, just before we had sat down to dinner. It was a line of text in quotation marks: *"If you want to understand your own country, then you've already stepped on the path to criminality,"* it read. And then: *Happy Spring Festival, comrades!*

A shiver ran through me. I logged off and walked back into the living room. Our parents sat on the couch, with Lulu on a stool beside them, their faces pallid in the television's flickering light as I joined them, stealing glances at this strange person, my twin sister.

The next day, the two of us went out to buy some ingredients for my mother: flour, fermented bean paste, ground pork. It felt odd to walk the half-mile to the supermarket together, the first time we'd been alone since she had visited me at college.

On the way, we passed a park where we used to play as children, and we could hear the sound of children there now. It was sunny, and the warmth lulled my skin.

"Where did that quote come from?" I said. "The one from last night."

She kept walking. "What do you mean?"

"I've been reading your account."

"I don't know what you're talking about." A man was walking by with a small dog, its face scrunched like the heel of a sausage, and Lulu nickered at it as it passed.

"Come on, Lulu." I stopped walking. "I'm worried about you."

She stopped a few feet ahead of me and stood there, not looking at me, arms crossed. "How did you know?"

I explained about the poetry. "Do other people know it's you?"

She shrugged. "A professor. Some other students." When I pressed her, she said reluctantly that a classmate had reported her to the department head, and that one of her professors had taken her aside and gently warned her that she should stop her activities online, lest it "influence" her future.

"They're right, you know," I said. "Don't you worry about how this might affect you?" One of the videos she'd posted, I remembered, showed a woman kneeling on the ground and wailing, "The government are traitors! The government doesn't serve the people!"

Lulu just stood there, staring at the little shopping complex opposite us as if she were trying to memorize it. There was a bilious orange fast-food restaurant, three test-prep centers, and two real estate agents' offices.

"Or our parents?" I said. They'd both retired by now, but each had a modest pension that I imagined could be taken away, and anyway, the ruining of Lulu's prospects would be the greatest loss of all. When I thought of having to support them on my own in their old age, my stomach creaked unhappily.

She nodded. "Of course," she said, finally. "I'm not stupid."

"So you'll stop, then?"

She looked at me for a moment, a little dreamily. "Did you know in the Song Dynasty it was illegal to throw away any pieces of paper with writing on them?" she said. "People had to go to certain temples with sacred fires set up where they could burn them instead. That's how much they revered the written word."

I wanted to shake her, but I didn't. "I don't see how that's relevant."

She started walking again.

"Where are you getting all this stuff?" I asked. She unbent slightly and explained that she had downloaded a tool that unblocked overseas websites. "It's not hard," she said. "But things get deleted quickly, so I have to keep reposting them."

"I had no idea these kinds of things went on," she added soberly. "We were lucky."

"We weren't rich."

"Dad worked for the government. We were comfortable."

Of course we were, I told her, but so were lots of people, and it didn't mean that she had to expose herself to trouble.

"It's better than just playing video games all day," she shot back, suddenly angry with me. "What's the point of that?"

I stuck my hands in my pockets and shrugged, taking a few extra breaths to calm myself. It was strange to see Lulu angry; she was usually so even-keeled. "Fair enough," I said. We kept walking, not looking at each other. Inside the supermarket we parted, as though with relief.

Back on campus, spring brought translucent white buds to the trees, like the tiny cores of onions. The birds grew noisy and self-righteous, clacking and clamoring at all hours outside my window, making it hard to sleep. Lulu had stopped posting, I was pleased to see. I began working part-time at a restaurant downtown that served large, expensive banquets, helping to prepare plates of cold chopped meats, glassy collagen, and frilly slices of cucumber dolled up to look like miniature peacocks. There was a rhythm and a repetition to the work that I liked, a sense of contentment in washing up at the night's end and putting things back where they belonged.

One day in May, just before graduation, I checked back in on my sister's account. Lulu had stopped updating her chat status: for several weeks, it had read simply *out,* and I'd grown worried.

It was as it had been months before: she'd gone back to posting frenetically, as though she'd lost control; in one day alone she had posted forty-three times. There were the same postcards of protests around the country, the videos and photographs she'd been sharing before, and a lot of simple text posts, too, one after another: 3:34 a.m.: *If this country were a vegetable, it would be a rotten, bitter melon.* 3:36 a.m.: *I am the daughter of a government sanitation worker. I know the smell of s——.* 3:37 a.m.: *I'm sorry, friends, just a little tired today after so many posts. There are many beautiful things, too, in this life.* And then she'd shared a series of pictures of small goats leaping in the air, tiny hoofs aloft against green grass. 3:41 a.m.: *Okay, I am sufficiently soothed to go to sleep. Good night, comrades, until tomorrow.*

The posts went on and on — thousands of them had accumulated in the time since I'd stopped checking. I scrolled through them with a mounting sense of horror, and then paged back up and felt my stomach flip: somehow she'd amassed 800,000 followers.

I messaged her frantically, fingers scrabbling at the keys. *Goats?*

A few hours later, she answered me. *Did you like them?*

They're okay.

I'm sorry, Big Brother. I couldn't stop.

I sat and watched the cursor blink, like a slow pulse.

A lot of people are paying attention to you. I couldn't tell if I should be proud of her, worried for her, or angry with her; I supposed I was all three.

Yes, they are. Another long silence. *Don't be upset, Big Brother. I just felt this was something I had to do. Don't you agree?*

I'm working now, I wrote her, hoping she could sense my anger. *Running late, got to go.*

After she graduated, Lulu moved in with her boyfriend, Zhang-wei, in Beijing. She started her own anonymous website, a constant stream of news about protests and human rights abuses around the country. There was the story of a woman, beaten to death by police, whose daughter had paid to keep her body frozen in a morgue for six years, unwilling to inter the evidence. There was the story of the village where officials had torn down an elderly grandmother's home in the middle of the night to make way for a shopping mall;

she'd been given no warning and had died in her bed as the roof collapsed. Each post carried its own mordant title: THE MOTHER POPSICLE; THE FRUSTRATED SLEEPER.

They came for her one night, to the third-floor apartment that she and Zhangwei were renting. They burst in through the door without warning and informed her, politely, that she should go with them. "The landlord must have given them the key," she told me later, stunned. It was that particular detail, oddly, that seemed to haunt her.

It was midnight when Lulu called me from the police van to say that she was being taken away. "Tell our parents," she said. "Please. I'm sorry." Her voice broke, and I barely recognized it. She sounded like a child in a blizzard who'd lost her scarf. It was easier to think of that than to think of the alternative: Lulu, cuffed into a van and taken away by four men who sneered at her for being un-married and living with her boyfriend, for trying to stir up trouble, for spreading rumors — a crime punishable by seven years' imprisonment.

When they began interrogating her, it was worse. "Did you go to any of these places?" they kept asking. "Did you confirm any of these things yourself before spreading these rumors online?"

No, Lulu said. No.

"So you didn't know if they were true, then."

Later, they laid her on the ground and kicked and beat her. They didn't fracture any bones, but I pictured her bones anyway, each individually absorbing every blow. Lulu would have known all of them by heart: sternum, tibia, floating rib.

I called my mother, who, on receiving the news, still half asleep, went blank. "You must be mistaken," she told me sharply. "Let me call Lulu to straighten things out." It was an old reflex of hers, this instinct to turn to her daughter.

"You can call; she won't answer," I said, but she'd already hung up. When I called back, my father took in the news helplessly, as though he'd been expecting it. I tried to explain the kinds of things Lulu had been writing, but he cut me off.

"Lulu is my daughter. I can imagine," he said. There was a particular heaviness in his voice that surprised me, and it made me think that maybe he'd known her better than the rest of us had.

Lulu was freed after six days and went back to her apartment to convalesce. We flew to Beijing the next day to see her. It was the first time I had been in her apartment, whose living-room wall bore a giant decal from a previous tenant, featuring silver and pink trees and a striped pink kitten. YOU ARE MY HAPPY SURPRISE, FRIENDS ARE BETTER IN AUTUMN, it read. Lulu's skin looked yellow and darkly bruised, and there was a dart of something red in her right eye that peeked out when she looked in certain directions.

"I'm all right," she said. She seemed acutely embarrassed to see us. They'd only wanted her to stop what she was doing, she said. She'd been a good student, one of the best in her class—she didn't have to ruin it all. It was a misunderstanding, she told us. They'd let her go, after all.

It seemed that she wanted us to go, too. We stayed for a week, our mother fussing in their tiny kitchen, preparing large meals of things sliced and intricately diced and cooked over a high flame. "I'm okay," Lulu said, until we stopped asking.

After we went home, Lulu started chatting me late at night, at odd hours. I was usually awake anyway. Since graduating, I'd moved back home to work in the kitchen at a local hotel. I spent my days chopping and rinsing, bleary-eyed, and my nights with teammates, locked in online combat. There was something that intensified in her messages during those months. She wanted to know how our parents were, if it was raining, if I'd eaten yet. She wondered if she could sue the police who'd beaten her; she'd been having stomach pains ever since. She wanted to know if I remembered the story of the mother who died in the hospital down the street from us before we were born. She wondered if there was any way to learn the fate of the dead mother's child today—had it lived, it would be about our age by now.

Soon after that, the posts on her site started up again, thick and fast. I watched with a sinking heart, trying to distract her. *When are you and Zhangwei getting married?* I tried. *Didn't you want to have a baby?*

Soon, she said. *Maybe.*

When the police came and took her away again, she was prepared; she got up quietly from the couch and went with them without a word, leaving her keys behind. This time when they allowed her access to a phone, she called a lawyer, not me. The police raided the apartment, taking her computer, the blue-sleeved laptop my parents had given her. They also left behind a notice saying that she was formally being arrested and charged.

At the trial, Lulu wore an orange jumpsuit, with hair shorn so short that she was barely recognizable. She stared straight ahead at the prosecutors, never once looking out at the audience. We'd flown out for the occasion; we hadn't seen her for six months. She was given a sentence of three years, then jerked away through a door at the opposite end of the courtroom, and that was all.

On the plane, my mother wept all the way home. "What more did she want?" she kept saying.

To her left, my father hushed her. "There's nothing we can do now," he said. The thought, strangely, appeared to console him.

Back at home no one seemed to know that anything had happened to my sister, and no one asked, either. It was as if a great white blanket of snow had descended, softly muffling everything in its path.

Time passed, and eventually I was made a sous chef at the hotel, with a modest raise and a new, slightly taller paper hat. When I felt restless or agitated, which was often, I'd log on and join my teammates online.

One night I brought my girlfriend home for the first time. I'd met her the month before on the lowest basement floor of a warrened-out block devoted to the sale of electronics: a fluorescent-lit maze of close-set booths selling secondhand phones, cases, speakers, and power banks. Her name was Mao Xin, and she was one of the few girls working behind the counters there. She could tell you the difference between 100 WH and 161 WH, could quote the price per gigabyte of different models; she'd spent so damn long in the shop figuring out which items were comparative junk, she confessed sheepishly, that she didn't see any point in stocking the others at all. "But then we'd just be selling maybe six things," she said with a frown.

As it turned out, she'd grown up riding the same bus route I had, and in a city as big as ours, that was enough to feel like fate.

We liked to imagine that we had seen each other on the bus as children, stiffly bundled in the winter or swinging our legs impatiently in the summer, had maybe even clung to the same pole.

Over dinner that night, as we sat and slurped potatoes stewed with ginger and pork, my mother quizzed Mao Xin. I could see that she wanted to like her, had observed the way she'd helped chop the garlic and cut the yellowing tips off the chives. Mao Xin exuded a kind of benevolent competence that soothed everyone, even my mother, who had grown jittery since Lulu's trial, prone to repeat herself, easily annoyed. Under Mao Xin's spell, I paced the apartment looking for things to do. I wiped away browning soap residue from the bathroom counter, and bundled and took out the trash without being asked.

As we talked, I could see Mao Xin's curious eyes flicking around, eventually landing on a photo of Lulu atop a bookshelf across the room, high enough that you needed to squint to really see it. "Who's that?"

"It's his sister," my father said. The photo had been taken the day she won our district's top score for math in the college entrance exam. In it she was grinning maniacally at my father behind the camera, a little out of focus.

"I didn't know you had a sister," she said to me. "She looks like you."

"They're twins," my father said.

"Where is she?"

"She's in the northeast, preparing to get her Ph.D.," my mother said.

Later, when I walked Mao Xin outside and explained what had

really happened, her face fell. "Oh," she said. "I'm so sorry." When she was growing up, she said, there was a man who used to station himself outside the government offices down the street from her home, with torn fatigues and sneakers so worn they flopped open like petals around his ankles. He'd tell anyone who would listen about how the army owed him seven years of back pay. He'd been there every day through her childhood, she said, until one day he disappeared for good.

"It sounds like he was crazy," I said.

"I think so," she said. "Maybe not at first, though."

"You must have been scared of him."

"More just sorry for him," she said.

We planned our wedding for a few days after Lulu was to be released from prison, a boisterous dinner in the nicest hall of the hotel where I worked. I'd been made a full chef there that month, which felt like a sort of wedding gift. We served big platters of cold jellied meats and swans made of mashed-up radishes, with carrot beaks and black sesame eyes. It should have been a happy occasion, and I guess it was, but whenever I looked at Lulu, sitting across from me with a distant look in her eyes, my heart caught in my throat.

As the banquet wound down, my father, unnatural in a rented tuxedo, began coughing violently. When he didn't stop, Zhangwei signaled to one of the waiters for water.

"Drink up," Lulu said. He drained the glass, almost angrily, it seemed. The coughs sputtered, subsided. "You're okay?" she said.

He had been drinking, his face was flushed, and his eyes focused suddenly on her, as though surprised she was there. "Do you think what you've done is meaningful?" he said.

"Let's not talk about it."

"You didn't even know these people," he said. "Whatever their problems might have been, they had no relation to you."

Lulu looked down at her plate, appearing not to hear. She'd grown adept at that while in prison, or maybe she'd always had that skill: how to sort the world into clear categories, what she thought was worth paying attention to, and what wasn't. I was in the latter category now. She'd nod at me occasionally and respond when spoken to, but that was all. I tried not to let it upset me.

My father's face was getting red; none of us had ever seen him like that before. "Dad, let's just leave it," I said. Guests at nearby tables had stopped their conversations, craning to hear. "It's no use."

"You are our daughter," he said fiercely, ignoring me. "Everything we could, we did for you. You were all our worries, all our hopes."

He was coughing again, small mangled noises sticking in his throat. Lulu's expression softened. "Dad, drink more water. It sounds like you're really sick."

He ignored her, setting the glass down in the same ring of condensation. He was suddenly an old man, or maybe I'd only just noticed. "Do you think I had your chances in life?" he said. "Do you know what I could have done if I had them?"

It was hard to believe that the two of them were fighting; it was something I hadn't seen before. Our mother and I looked at each other, then looked away.

"I'm sorry," Lulu said quietly.

"You want to help people, Lulu, but don't deceive yourself," he said. "All you've done is hurt yourself, hurt your family."

My mother laid a hand on his and stilled him with a look. Zhangwei stood up, as though to end the discussion. It made you aware of what a tall, fine-looking man he was, stiff black hair that stood up in a dense thatch, thin lenses highlighting watchful brown eyes. "I think Lulu had better get some rest now," he said to my parents. There was nothing impolite about his tone, but there was a finality to it that reminded us all of his solidity, his determination to protect my sister, and I liked him the better for it.

"Don't worry," he told me as he ushered her outside, away from the noise and lights of the wedding party. "I'll take care of her."

She hadn't been treated badly in prison, she'd said when we were all first gathered again in our parents' living room. There had been a female guard she suspected of having a crush on her, who used to smuggle her packets of instant noodles and an occasional stick of gum. During the day they'd work on a manufacturing line, assembling Christmas lights. At night they'd watch the evening news and whatever sports match was being televised. But she'd missed the sunlight, she said. She'd missed Zhangwei, missed us.

"Thank you for your letters," she said to me, and I looked at the floor, away from our parents. "It was no problem," I muttered, embarrassed for them. It hadn't occurred to me that they hadn't been writing regularly as well.

Lulu changed the subject. "So you're playing in the Shanghai invitational? That's really wonderful."

It was: after playing together for six years, my team had finally qualified. Out of four teammates, I'd met only one in person thus far. I thanked her.

"Is there prize money?" she asked.

I told her yes, a little.

"Excellent," she said, grinning.

Our parents were very quiet. I suspected they wanted an apology, and also that it wasn't forthcoming. When Lulu said that she and Zhangwei were planning to move nearby, our mother froze, as though she'd been handed a cracked egg and didn't know what to do with it.

"He thinks it'll be good for me to be closer to home," Lulu said, breaking the silence. "At least while I get used to a normal life again."

"What can you do out here?" my mother asked stiffly. "Can you find work?"

Lulu tossed her head, and a flash of her old arrogance flared in her. "Yes, Mother. I was the top-scoring student in our year for math, don't you remember?"

"Maybe Mao Xin could give her a job," my mother said. It wasn't a tactful remark, but then my mother loved Mao Xin, had come to rely on her in a way that reminded me of her relationship with Lulu before she had gone to college.

"Sure," I said, with an apologetic glance at Lulu. "Anyway, that's great news. We'll have to celebrate."

She smiled at me, a little sadly. "Thanks, Big Brother."

Eventually she found work handing out tea samples at the mall, a chain store with neon-green hills on its sign. It was an easy job, and the boss didn't ask questions about her past. In the meantime she was learning a lot about tea, she said, about the oxidation process, about the proper way to steep different varieties.

"Wow, they really train you over there," our father said. In the weeks since her release, he had become a champion government booster, missing no opportunity to point out to Lulu how nicely the roads had been paved since she'd left, how grand the malls were that had been built. "There are so many opportunities for young people now," he said. It was a new tic of his, and it grated. Earlier that day, as we strolled the neighborhood, he'd pointed out a set of recently upgraded public toilets across the way. "They even installed a little room where the sanitation workers can rest," he said. "It has heating and everything. You see what good care they take of all the workers now?"

I rolled my eyes.

"Anyway, it's temporary," Lulu said of her job, and that, of course, is what scared us most of all.

I could see that she was planning something. Once, when she was using my laptop, I saw over her shoulder that she had a document open, titled "An Open Letter to the National People's Congress." When she got up to use the bathroom, I scrolled hastily through the text, seeing a list of half a dozen names signed, her own and those of a few lawyers and professors, no one I'd ever heard of. I didn't say anything to her, but later that afternoon I pulled Zhangwei aside and told him what I'd found. He nodded.

"I know," he said. "Your sister doesn't change."

I didn't know what he meant, but I bristled a little anyway. "She wasn't like this when she was younger," I said.

"Of course not — she was too young then."

"You don't know what she was like."

"Okay," he said patiently, his eyes on the door behind me, waiting to see if Lulu would walk in. He was always mentally tracking her location, the world's most devoted bloodhound.

"I mean that. She was smart. She was probably the smartest in our school."

"And you think she isn't smart anymore?"

"That's not what I meant," I said, but Zhangwei was already flicking the ash from his cigarette and walking away, disappointed in me.

I flew to Shanghai for the midseason invitational alone, shrugging off Mao Xin's offer to accompany me, but when I arrived I immediately wished she was there, just to see the spectacle. The games took place in a stadium downtown, the floor lit up with strips of red and blue LED lights. The stadium was packed, and as we played in padded seats onstage, headsets on, the crowds waved red and blue glow sticks.

We won two rounds and went on to trounce the South Korean team in the third. In the background, the crowd was moaning, their sounds mingling with the noise of my own blood as we clicked frantically, sending out great gusts of orange fire. "Never give up! Never say die!" the crowd chanted.

When the games were over, the flashing scoreboard had us in third place. The cameras flocked to the floor, descending on us like black hooded birds. We gave sheepish smiles and said how proud we were, how we'd be back next year to win for sure. Somehow we were ushered onto a podium, beside the other winning teams. They handed us a trophy as silver confetti rained down, great clouds of delicate parallelograms. When I watched the video later, it looked as if we were standing in a hail of razor blades. We hoisted the trophy into the air, all five of us. It wavered and nearly tipped, but the tallest among us righted it and we let it hover there, admiring it.

Four months later Lulu went back to prison, this time on charges of trying to subvert state power, after she had circulated an online petition calling for all government spending to be made transparent. This time the prison was not so nice, and the judge gave her a ten-year sentence. The last time I saw her, she had lost fifteen pounds and looked shrunken, the same size she'd been in high school.

A few years after she was jailed, Zhangwei moved back to his hometown to be closer to his parents and got married to someone else. He wrote us a letter apologizing. I threw it away after seeing the return address, but Mao Xin fished it out of the trash and insisted that I read it. "Your sister is a truly rare person, and it is with the greatest sadness that I have to move on," he'd written. "I'm sorry I couldn't help her more." I stood there for a minute, admiring his penmanship, which I'd never seen before. It was elegant, balanced—almost noble, I observed, before tossing the letter out again.

After the Shanghai invitational, our team started competing heavily on the domestic circuit, winning actual prize pools now and again. With Mao Xin's encouragement, I cut back my hours at the hotel and devoted more time to training. The following summer, we flew to Sydney for the global finals. It was my first time abroad. By then we had fans, even sponsors; we entered the arena wearing identical jumpsuits with the name of an energy drink printed across our chests.

On the plane, we crossed the ocean, heading south. I took out my camera and snapped a photo for my next letter to Lulu. The flight attendants passed out headsets and I slid one on, suddenly homesick. I closed my eyes and thought of my sister. I prayed for victory, and hoped that she would be proud.

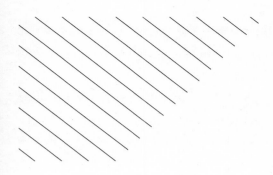

HOTLINE GIRL

THE HIGHWAYS WERE ADORNED WITH THOUSANDS OF ROSES EACH SPRING. They came in bright pinks and butter yellows, perfect potted visions in the center meridian. The annual choreography of thorns and petals usually came in April, after the winter gloom lifted. During those dark and choking months, the authorities painted the roads a luminous yellow: *For better cheer and energy during the gray!* The bulletins came like that, dozens of them a day:

Attention, they said. *This afternoon, shorthair kittens* (and they would appear onscreen, big-pawed and blinking, and commuters would look up and smile).

Attention: how maple syrup is made (a man in a stark forest drilling into a tree, gray vats of boiling liquid).

Attention: the ginkgo leaves are turning gold around Nanshan Park—come see!

And so on.

When Bayi stepped out that morning, like every morning, she slipped a red lanyard with her identification card around her neck. The lanyard's color confirmed her status as a resident of the city, hard-won after years of jobs at its margins. The card had her picture and name and work unit on it. Anyone entering the city had to wear one. Each card synced with the city's sensors and recorded the bearer's activity. At the end of the day, you could log on and see the number of miles you'd walked; it was one of the system's more popular features.

"I'm going on a highway, I'm going on a lightning bolt," she sang as she walked to the subway. For years she'd wanted to be a singer, tried to make her voice the strong, slender vessel she wanted it to be, tried to write a breakout hit. They were short melodies, just a few refrains repeated on a loop; she couldn't seem to figure out how to write a full one, chorus, verse, bridge.

The trains were packed that morning. All the stations piped in classical music at rush hour; it was supposed to soothe tempers, but everyone still pushed and elbowed one another. Bayi distrusted it instinctively, anyway; all those long, meandering phrases—it felt like cheating. She wanted her music precise, to have a point.

When she'd pushed her way through the crowds, up the elevator seven floors, and into the office, she could see the oily bristles of Qiaoying's hair over his screen. "I had a plumber come this morning," she said, shrugging, as he stood and frowned at her. "They're always running late."

She didn't apologize. She'd realized early on apologies were the surest way for Qiaoying to decide that you were *ruan shizi,* soft fruit, easily picked on. The other girls didn't get that. They kept their eyes lowered, almost visibly leaning away as he passed their stations. One girl would spring up and hide in the bathroom any time he approached their corridor, the one that bore a sign saying HOTLINE GIRLS.

"We've already had twenty-seven calls," her friend Suqi whispered to her. They both looked automatically at the girl sitting at the row's end and sighed. The girl, Juanmei, had been picked as this year's office Model Worker. It wasn't clear why, except that she had pleasing features and long hair that fell in a silky black rain about her face. For months her glowing image had blanketed the subway and billboards across town: WARM, GENTLE, CAPABLE: GOVERNMENT WORKERS CAN HELP YOU RESOLVE ANY QUESTION, ANY CONCERN. CALL THE SATISFACTION OFFICE TODAY: 12579.

When the switchboard pinged, no one looked to Juanmei anymore. Ever since her award she'd been slack, creating more work for the other girls. All calls had to be answered within forty-five seconds. All chats had to be replied to within twenty seconds. It meant that while Juanmei was sitting idly there with her headset on, Bayi and the others were scrambling, picking up, pressing *hold*, picking up, muttering, pressing *return* on their keyboards, typing fast. When she first came to the city, Bayi had worked for a time in fast food. It was that same complicated kind of dance, keeping ten orders in your head simultaneously, twirl, turn about, begin again.

The switchboard pinged once more as Bayi opened up her chat screen and faced a barrage of popups. The easiest thing was to send a smiley face. She started all her conversations that way. There were set programmed keys for smiley faces, and another key that spat out: *Hello, Satisfaction Office, what can I help you with?*

The switchboard kept pinging, the big timer with its red numerals counting down. If no one picked up by the time the number hit zero, a buzzer sounded and everyone's rating was docked. Still, the other girls didn't budge; they were waiting for her to take the call. Everyone knew she'd just arrived. She jerked on her headset irritably. "Hello, Satisfaction Office, what can I help you with?"

A swarm of words enveloped her ear, a raspy connection. It sounded like the person was dialing from a rooftop on a windy day.

"Excuse me, I didn't catch that . . . You want a housing—I'm sorry, please restate the matter. You've been evicted?" She was guessing now, half the time you could fill in the blanks yourself. There were complaints about corrupt officials, questions about social subsidies. There were all the lonely people who dialed the government day after day, wanting to talk, the elderly or mentally infirm, many with complaints that would never be resolved. One mother called regularly to inquire about a daughter who had gone missing ten years before: kidnapped, she was sure. One agitated

man called their office for months, complaining there were ter-
mites in the tree opposite his building; he was convinced they'd get
into the wires and electrocute the neighborhood. They'd sent an
inspector, who'd found nothing. They'd sent someone who'd pretended to spray, to set his heart at rest, but it didn't satisfy him. At
last they'd sent someone to chop the whole thing down, and he
stopped calling.

"Excuse me, not a housing—you want to report someone? . . .
An unregistered kitchen knife? Let me take that down."

She began typing, simultaneously pressing the button for *Tell
me more* on four different windows that popped up. One woman was
complaining about a court verdict, saying the judge was related
to the defendant. Another man claimed authorities were illegally
taxing his restaurant. A senior said he hadn't been getting the rise
in pension payments he was owed.

Her shoulders were starting to ache and she rubbed her eyes,
staring out at the sea of computers around her. It always surprised
her how quickly time passed, taking down notes, sending links,
marking case urgency by color. A few times Bayi routed red com-
passion packets to callers, just to smooth things over; there was a
common budget for that, for the particularly obstreperous cases
who refused to hang up. "I'm going to report you to your super-
vising agency—oh, I just received a notification—thank you for
your good intentions. No, I know you are only trying to help." It
was astonishing how many residents just needed to feel they'd ex-
tracted something, anything, from the other end of the line, even
if it was only 10 or 20 yuan.

At noon the deliveryman arrived outside and unloaded two

hundred boxed lunches, white containers of rice or noodles with vegetables and shredded pork. The options were nearly identical but everyone crammed the narrow hall in a frantic rush anyway, the grease turning the cardboard orange and translucent.

As they waited, Suqi stretched out her leg and showed off one boot, and she and Bayi squealed. "You got them!"

"I did," Suqi said proudly. "Do you think I'm crazy?"

"A little," Bayi said. The boots were knitted from soft brown leather, studded with the whorls of tiny seashells, and cost a month's salary. Suqi had the office's highest bonuses; her satisfaction rate was extraordinary, and she almost never got repeat callbacks. It wasn't because she used the red packets, either; there was just something so reasonable and capable in Suqi's manner — she never argued and had an encyclopedic knowledge of the government's workings, knew just what resources she could offer, was genuinely good at helping people. She was a hard worker, too: in the evening she picked up extra shifts working in transport.

The call came around 2 p.m., when they'd settled back into their stations, into that midday stretch when calls ebbed and it was hard to keep your eyes open. One of the girls on the line kept a spray bottle nearby, periodically misting her face to stay alert. Bayi was feeling lazy, dealing with some chats by simply sending a nodding face, which bought another minute before you had to reply again.

The switchboard pinged, and Bayi waited until the timer showed ten seconds left, then punched firmly and straightened up. "Hello, Satisfaction Office, what can I help you with?"

There was a silence. She spoke again, impatiently. "Hello?" and "Hello?"

Bayi frowned into the receiver. Occasionally, very rarely, you'd get a heavy breather. Sometimes they might say inappropriate things: ask what you were wearing, if you were married, had a boyfriend.

She was about to hang up when she heard a voice: "Wow, at last."

"I'm sorry?"

"Bayi. It's me."

She sat back, pulled her headset away for a moment and cupped the earpiece, eyes closed. Then, when she'd composed herself, she put it back again. "Yes, sir. Why are you—I mean, please state the matter," she said.

"I called probably sixty times already today," he said. "I wasn't sure I'd ever get you."

She looked around to the other girls on the line and spoke neutrally. "Is there something I can help you with?"

There was a silence. "Is that it?" he said.

"This is a government line," she said coldly. "Is there a matter that requires assistance?"

"Yes," he said. "I wish you would see me. I'm here, I'm standing outside."

Bayi hung up automatically, the way one might drop a shoe at the sight of a cockroach scuttling inside. She breathed in, went back to her screen and picked up two more calls in a hurry: an abused wife, a man complaining about trash in his neighborhood. At 5 p.m., she slipped the lanyard about her neck again and exited through the service elevator around the back, moving fast, trying not to be seen.

She went home shakily, fixed herself a meal. She felt agitated all evening, like a hummingbird was trapped in her chest. At last, she went and paced outside for a while before sitting on the bench opposite the trash cans. After twenty minutes, one of the alley cats came up and snaked itself into her lap, and she petted it automatically. She stared into the bushes accusingly, as though they might conceal someone watching her.

The next day he called again.

"It was too much," he said. "I shouldn't have come over. I was just so excited to have found you."

She cleared her throat. "I wasn't lost."

"No, of course not," he said.

They were both silent. He had never been good at making conversation, she remembered. Sometimes they'd eat their meals together in almost complete silence, which, oddly, never seemed to bother him. She relaxed a little. There had always been an art to being around Keju. It meant turning off your mind, like lifting weights or falling asleep. It didn't feel as bad as it sounded. It was important to be strong, it was important to sleep; you needed both to stay alive.

"You're here?" she said. "I mean, I know you were yesterday. Are you visiting, or —?"

The city was 32 million people, none of whom were Keju; he should have been six hundred miles away.

"Just visiting," Keju said hastily, as though to reassure her.

They were silent again, and she watched her screen light up and flash. "I really can't talk now," she said.

"Don't hang up," he said. "It took me two hours to reach you today. Isn't there a direct line I can call, to know that you'll pick up?"

"It doesn't work that way."

"You're the Satisfaction Office, aren't you?" he said, trying to make a joke of it. "I'm not going to be satisfied until I get to talk to you."

She silently clicked over to another call and transferred it to the government's legal division. A few minutes later, he was still there.

"I do have complaints, you know," he said. "I could tell you about them."

"Fine." She opened a form.

"They tore down the old schoolhouse," he said. "They brought in a wrecking ball."

She knew the building, could picture it. He'd brought her there shortly after they'd started dating, on their first trip together to his old village. It was a small abandoned schoolhouse, just two rooms, something out of a historical photograph. They'd wandered it hand in hand, their voices strange in the empty rooms. For months afterward they used it as their private meeting spot. No one attended school in places like that anymore; actually, no one really lived in places like that anymore, with their bad roads and tiny dried-out plots of cultivated land. By the time he was growing up, Keju's family was one of the last holdouts, poor and very proud.

"I don't remember it," she lied.

"Are you sure?" he said, and his voice was teasing. "I know I do."

She felt the heat rise in her cheeks. "Not a real complaint," she said. "Next."

"I just want to see you, Bayi."

She made a noncommittal noise.

"I have another," he said.

"Okay." She sent a smiley face to a new chat. She copied instructions on how to file a whistleblower report into another window that was flashing repeatedly, and hit *send*.

"My parents aren't doing well," he said. "My father's spirits have been bad ever since we were relocated. I think the government should do something about it."

"Like a doctor."

"Not like a doctor. He's seen doctors."

"Like what, then?"

"I was thinking compensation." She raised her eyebrows. This was new. Keju's family had been relocated from the countryside a decade ago, when he was fourteen, to a city twenty miles west of their old home. It wasn't far, but it might as well have been another nation. It was a million people living in closely set blocks, with bus lines and supermarkets; it was parks with water features that lit up and sprayed arcs on the hour. It was where the two of them had met, back when they were in high school.

"I'm sorry to hear he's not doing well," she said, and she was. She had always liked Keju's father. He was obsessed with collecting gourds. He'd started the habit back in their village, and in the city, where he struggled to find work, it had become a fixation. Their apartment had two black bookshelves filled almost wholly with gourds, big ones like water bottles, small ones like toy tops, a few painted, others carved. Some he'd carved himself.

"There's a two-year statute of limitations for petitions on relocation compensation," she said, frowning a little. "You might try one of the spirit management committees; they often have subsidies he could apply for. You should call his local satisfaction office," she said. "They'll help you."

"Thank you," he said.

"I'm sorry I can't do more," she said, and meant it. She had liked his family. She liked the way his mother made their kitchen fragrant, dicing red and green bell peppers into pixels, mixing them with ground pork and bits of chopped vermicelli for lunch. She liked the way his father knew the seasons, how squash grew and how to pick the kinds of melons that were sweetest—she'd had no idea they came in male and female specimens (the female ones, with their slight dimple up top, were sweeter).

"That's okay," Keju said. He sounded sad. Toward the end, even when he'd struck her (never so hard, nothing requiring a doctor; there were girls who'd had it worse), he'd been so terminally sad and sorry afterward that she found herself patting his hand, making shushing noises, promising they'd get through it, which of course she knew was a lie, because even then she knew that Keju was a toxic piece of sea kelp that was going to cling and cling to her, that she needed to escape, even if it meant cutting off the limb he clung to. Still, she missed his family.

Her screen was flashing with unanswered messages; out of the corner of her eye she saw Qiaoying starting to rise. "I really have to go," she said desperately. "Please stop calling. It hurts my rating whenever someone calls back so quickly. Call your local satisfaction office, okay?"

"Bayi, would you just hold on a moment?" His voice was getting exasperated now, bladed.

"I hope you enjoy your time here," she added hurriedly.

"There's a movie tonight on the screens. You can watch it in the Central Square. Check your phone for the bulletins."

"Bayi—"

"Thanks so much. Goodbye!"

After work, she rode her scooter with some of the other girls to the mall downtown. There was a military parade scheduled for the next day, which meant the government had cleared the roads in advance and all the streets were long, glorious stretches of empty asphalt that they could ride their scooters down and feel like queens, could do zigzags all over if they pleased. A warm sunset light caught the steel and glass of the buildings and encased them in gold.

At the mall, they ate Korean food and stopped into one of the dozens of photo parlors that rented rooms by the hour. They were full of different props and costumes, giant foam dumplings and purple ruched gowns, cartoon cat masks and colorful parasols, a little dingy but cheap, and you could swap in and out different backgrounds, a green lagoon, a floodlit stage, a ballroom, whatever you wanted. The girls squeezed into one room and took repeated shots of one another, Bayi dressed as a feudal princess, Suqi as a tiger.

She hadn't told anyone about Keju, or about the animals. There was the time, six months after they'd started dating, that she'd come across a dead mouse in a box in his room. It was soft and slumped and gray, stiff-limbed, front crusted with blood: someone had partially severed one of its legs.

When she'd confronted Keju, he'd said it was just a mouse, it was going to be killed as part of a school science experiment. He'd given it a few days of freedom but he couldn't keep it, and so he'd had to kill it; it was only humane. The explanation was disturbing but possibly logical, and so she'd tried to put the thought aside.

Then there was the neighbor's dog. It was a shaggy golden creature with no neck, like a shark, and eyes usually half-closed in slumber, a somnolent thing. Once, they'd been sitting in the courtyard downstairs and she'd been cooing at it, scratching its ears. "You like that dog better than me, don't you?" Keju had said, and when she hadn't responded fast enough, he'd planted one boot on its neck and pushed, laughing. The dog squeaked. It made a raspy noise in its throat, guttural, whining. Bayi had pleaded for him to stop, and at last, he did. "Relax," he'd said. "I wasn't going to hurt him." After that, every time he saw the dog he kicked at it, casually, as though aiming at a stray soccer ball, just to tease her.

A few months later, one of the semi-feral cats that lurked outside of their high school had been lying on the asphalt, Keju stroking it, until it had startled and bitten him, drawing blood. Keju had talked jokingly of getting revenge on the cat for days, and everyone had rolled their eyes (he liked the attention), until one afternoon he'd pulled Bayi aside and showed her a steak knife. "I'm going to get that cat," he'd said, eyes glinting.

"You're crazy," she said.

"It attacked me first," he said.

"It's a *cat*," she said.

It didn't matter. He'd chased the cat around, knife in hand, alternately waggling his fingers, trying to get it to approach, and lunging at it. Bayi had watched him, near tears. She'd finally walked away. The next day she saw the cat, unhurt, but a week later it disappeared. Keju didn't volunteer any information, and she didn't ask. It was easy to imagine what he would say: "We're all animals," something stupid like that.

Then there was that time at the movies when he thought she was flirting with another boy and he'd turned mean and shaken her, savagely. That was how it began. From that day on, something changed between them. One day at lunch in front of his friends, he'd flipped up his own shirt and said, "Look, she's as flat as I am," and laughed. A week later, she'd teased him about the way he often ran his fingers through his hair, a nervous tic of his, and he'd struck her across the cheek. Each time, he'd get flustered, apologize, occasionally weep. "I didn't mean it, you just upset me," he'd say. "You're the best thing that's ever happened to me."

She wasn't brave enough to break it off with him. Instead, after she left home to pursue her ambitions as a singer, she gradually stopped answering his calls, or returning his messages. Eventually she'd heard that he'd dropped out of school.

The phone rang again at the office, two days later.

"I'm leaving tomorrow," Keju said. "I wanted to let you know."

"Okay," she said, idly composing a pattern of flowers and smiley faces on her screen, which she planned to send to the next recipient who messaged her. Sometimes she made impossibly elaborate bouquets of different flowers: tulips, sunflowers, roses, peonies. She liked to send those to elderly recipients in particular, liked to imagine their wrinkled faces softening and smiling to see them; it broke up the monotony of the day.

"I don't have anything else to do this afternoon," he said. "I'll wait outside your office."

And then, when she didn't reply: "Don't be like that, Bayi. I came a long way."

She let one of her chat windows sit idle for more than a minute, considering, and her screen flashed red angrily. She swore softly under her breath.

"Bayi?"

"What?"

"Please. Just let me buy you a coffee. I won't call you again."

"You promise?" she said.

"I promise."

They met that evening after work, in the plaza of the mall across the way. The plaza's fountain was activated, and kids were skipping in and out of it, screaming. "I never understood what was so fun about that," Bayi said, just to have something to say. Now that Keju was there, he stood silently, eyeing her. He was shorter than she remembered, and stockier. He wore cheap sunglasses and a sky-blue shirt, boxy and too short.

It struck her that something seemed wrong with him, and as he turned to face her she saw he was missing his right arm. "Oh," she said, surprised, then stopped herself. The sleeve that would have held his right arm was folded over and fastened with a safety pin, like a doll's blanket.

He caught her gaze and looked away. "An accident," he said.

"I see. It's been so long," she said, trying to cover her shock.

"Thanks for coming," he said.

"That's okay," she said uneasily, keeping her distance. "Did you want to get something to drink?"

They stopped at a stall and drank a lemonade in the fading light. She paid. Standing there, he felt familiar in the way of a distant cousin, or an old school acquaintance: full-fledged in her memory, but a stranger. She tried not to look at the blank space beside his body.

"So why are you here?" she asked.

"I'd never been before," he said, and she nodded as though it were an answer.

She fidgeted, scanning the scene around them, half wondering if any of her coworkers were nearby, watching. "Do you still keep up with anyone from school?" she said inanely. "I keep meaning to go back to visit." For a while she'd thought of visiting the music teacher who'd encouraged her talents, though enough time had passed that she wondered if he'd remember her.

Keju didn't reply: his eyes kept crisscrossing her, absorbing her. It made her feel acutely conscious of the shape of her clothes, the way her belt held her about her waist, the exposed parts of her feet in their sandals.

"You look different," he said. "You look nice."

She thanked him. "Keju, what happened to you?"

He was watching her steadily. Up close she could see the stubble on his chin, the bags under his eyes. There were lines around his mouth and on his neck that hadn't been there before. The sight of them made her feel suddenly sorrowful, aware of the miles and years that had passed.

"It was a factory explosion," he said. "A fire."

"I'm so sorry." She could picture it: the orange fireball going up into the sky, shaky footage shot by residents; there were accidents like that every few weeks, places that had been neglected, factory inspectors paid off, planning studies that had never been done. Always the same reasons.

"The place hadn't been inspected in four years," he said. "We were locked in during our shift. It was a firetrap."

She shook her head sympathetically. Out of habit, she found herself wanting to tell him it was something that was being addressed, that there were government programs and new laws being drafted, but the words died on her lips.

"Might have been worse," he said. "I almost didn't make it. Hid in the crawl space for hours."

Fire isn't something to hide from, she thought, but couldn't bring herself to speak. She didn't know what she could say around him anymore. After they'd parted ways it surprised her how quickly he'd faded from her life, as did the absence of news of him from mutual friends. It occurred to her later that she had been one of very few who'd been close to him, perhaps the only one.

"I panicked," he said. "Didn't even notice how much time had gone by. It felt like I'd never be able to move again."

He was standing with his back to the screen above the square, which was lit with a swirling orange spiral, as though the sun were rising out of his head. *Doesn't it matter that you are one of a billion plus?* an announcer was saying, an advertisement of some kind. *It doesn't matter — you are one of us.*

"After you cut me off, I went a little crazy. Dropped out of school," he said. "You never told me what I did wrong."

Bayi opened her mouth to speak, then paused. "It was so long ago," she said. There was a steady drift of the crowd moving toward the screen. In another twenty minutes, the dance party would start. The districts held them every evening; they were free and principally attended by retirees, everyone shimmying together in a choreographed group. This week, the bulletins had said, the theme was Caribbean.

"We were good together," he said. He drained his lemonade through the straw, and the sound of it made her wince. Behind him in the distance, kids chased one another, shrieking. She wondered if he was able to tie his shoes, drive a car, cut a piece of meat.

"Do you ever think about those days?" he said, and reached out and cupped her face with his hand, rough to the touch. She tried not to recoil or move and instead stared straight ahead, holding her breath.

"Please don't," she said, voice cracking.

He didn't seem to hear: his hand was in her hair now, fingering her scalp. He leaned in as though for a kiss, tenderly murmuring her name, until she recalled herself and jerked away.

"No," she said, more forcefully than she meant to.

His face was that of a child who'd been struck, and for a moment she regretted her reaction. But then Keju turned to face the plaza's screen, and she saw his face smooth and rearrange itself, as though nothing had happened. He was proud. It was something she'd always liked about him.

They watched the crowd silently: a distant sound of drumbeats was starting up. Out of the corner of her eye, she could see him looking at her, but she stared determinedly ahead.

"Anyway, I'm glad I got to see you," he said finally, as though the city had a set number of attractions and she was on the list.

"It's nice here, isn't it?" she said, relenting.

He looked beyond her: it was a pleasant scene, the kids running around, the crowds of retirees in their bright skirts and sequined tops, getting ready to dance. On the perimeter were the black-uniformed security officers, a couple of them casually talking with tourists crossing the plaza, a few speaking into walkie-talkies.

"To be honest, it gives me the creeps," Keju said.

"I guess it takes getting used to," she said stiffly. She looked at the lanyard strung around his neck, its green cord and green badge the size of a soap dish clearly identifying him as a non-resident. The photo of him was scarcely recognizable, his face sallow, too broad, its proportions badly rendered to fit the badge; it made him look like a much older man.

"You should really call your local satisfaction office," she said. "I hope your dad will be okay."

Keju was silent for a few minutes, staring at the fountain. "You always thought you were too good for everything," he said. "You were going to be this great singer, remember?"

She shut her eyes, briefly. "I remember."

"Now look at you, taking calls all day in a cubicle," he said, his voice harsh. "All alone in this big city. Really, Bayi, I'm sorry for you."

Strains of Caribbean music were starting to drift to them, some of the black-uniformed police were handing out maracas. They finished their lemonade and lapsed into a strained silence, which finally she broke. "I've got to go, Keju." There wasn't anything else to say. "Good luck with everything," she said.

After they parted, Bayi couldn't bring herself to go underground, not quite yet. She'd walk awhile, she decided. Her parents, she thought, would have liked her to marry him. There was something quietly dependable about him: once when he was away on a holiday and the networks were down he'd walked two miles to find a place to call and say good night to her. "You'll never find anyone who loves you so much," she remembered her mother saying. If they'd married, too, it would have meant that Bayi would've stayed at home, wouldn't have been a single girl in the capital, taking calls from who only knew—of course it was a good job, a government job, but still.

There was a bulletin on her phone that had popped up moments after they'd finished their lemonade. *Attention,* it ran: *learn the five things to do before bedtime to wake up refreshed.* She turned her attention to the screen and watched as a beautiful woman cut the stems off a quartet of ruby-red strawberries and rinsed them at a sink.

A few blocks later, someone shouted and she looked up. It was Suqi, sitting at the steering wheel of a large van, window rolled down, grinning.

It was an unmarked government van. Anyone could tell it was intended for the discontented, the protesters who tried to stir up trouble, usually from out of town. It had all the subtle signs: the missing license plate, the large man staring stolidly ahead in the front passenger's seat, the metal grill separating Suqi from her human cargo, bound for a nearby detention center. The backseat windows were tinted, but through the windshield she could see the seats were mostly filled.

"You want a ride?" Suqi said, gesturing to the backseat.

Bayi forced a laugh. "Shut up," she said, and kept walking.

"Have it your way," Suqi said, and stuck out her tongue, a little fillip of pink. Bayi smiled back and watched her drive off. She'd go home, she thought, put her feet in some hot water, maybe watch something. She was glad to be off work, glad it was spring. It was good, she thought, to be young, to have a weekend, to be free.

NEW FRUIT

IT WAS A PECULIAR FRUIT: THE ORANGE-RED TAWNY SKIN, ITS FLESH DENSE AND VELVETY AND LUXURIOUS. It was shaped roughly like an egg, with a tiny yellow pit, sold packed into crates lined with its deeply green leaves.

The fruit had a taste marvelous and rare, sweet with an underside of acid. We lined up for blocks to buy it from street peddlers. We exchanged bites, though never satisfactorily. What tasted to me like the look of freshly arranged sunflowers in a green vase might taste to you like the way your daughter's tiny socked feet sounded romping down the hall.

For Lao Zhou, it smelled like it did when he wiped the shavings off a bench he'd carved himself, and applied a creamy varnish. For Zhu Ayi, it was the scent of her mother cooking rice, long-remembered from childhood, and the sound of rain outside. For others it was the look of mingled envy and admiration that came when you were young, and beautiful, and wearing something new that suited you exactly.

The fruit had arrived one day in trucks at the city's wholesale market in crates that said SUNSHAN PRODUCE, sharing space with peaches and plums and grapes and other fruit with which we were more familiar. At first it was just the peddlers who sold the fruit —who'd picked it up because it was cheap and novel and sweet —but soon grocery stores were stocking it, too, under the name *qiguo,* peculiar fruit.

Lao Zhou was the first on the street to try it. He was a widower who woke early every morning and did his shopping, was usually among the first at the neighborhood market. One day in April, he came back with a dozen of the fruit swaying in a plastic bag and handed them to anyone he saw. "Try it," he said, an alertness in his voice that surprised us.

Pang Ayi, out for a stroll, took one curiously. The first bite made her cheeks burn softly pink. "Oh," she said. "Oh, how tasty." Those of us who stood watching the exchange between her and Lao Zhou raised our eyebrows. There was something private in that moment, even though Pang Ayi was frequently found gossiping while squatting in the common privies and it would not have occurred to us, to any of us, to suspect her of holding anything in reserve.

It had been an especially frigid winter, months of chapped lips and living off stocks of stewed cabbage, months in which we had turned up our coat collars and nodded to one another in passing and kept to ourselves and turned the television up high. By the time the *qiguo* arrived, spring was just making itself felt, and it was a relief to shed our coats and walk unencumbered.

Those of us who ate the *qiguo* noticed that the sun was warm on our limbs and the sound of a bicycle bell tinkling outside reminded us of the warm air, of the spring breeze, of possibilities. We smiled more often, let our eyes meet in the street. "Today I had one that tasted like I had just told a good joke and everyone was laughing," Lao Sui might say. Mothers would feed mashed-up pieces of the fruit to their babies and we'd crowd around to watch the surprise and wonder that transformed their small faces.

We were kinder to one another that season. Mr. Feng, who worked at a local bank, tasted a *qiguo* one morning and afterward it occurred to him that the metal door at the entrance to the apartment building was sticking, so that the elderly woman who lived on the first floor could sometimes be seen standing outside, waiting for a neighbor to enter or exit so she could slip in behind them. He grabbed some pliers and went downstairs to see whether he could fix it.

Other changes happened, big and small. To everyone's astonishment, Zhu Ayi's son, who lived with her on the third floor, quit his job at a local factory and moved south to be a painter; he had taken a bite of the *qiguo* and (so he said) seen a sunset of moist silver and cloudy gold that he was determined to capture on canvas, no matter (so his mother said) that he had no talent and would come to a bad end.

Lao Zhou, who worked as the neighborhood handyman, was often seen eating the fruit. That spring, he found himself singing more often as he swung his hammer, feeling a long-dormant restlessness in his blood. He noticed the young girls in the neighborhood were wearing high-waisted skirts; it seemed to be the new fashion. He noticed the far-off sound of a revving engine in the distance. The day he'd given Pang Ayi her first piece of the fruit, he noticed that the shape of her waist was still visible, even in the baggy shirts she wore now, and though they had known each other for years, there was a freshness about her eyes that surprised him. For the first time it occurred to him, tasting the *qiguo,* that he was not yet an old man.

The only one on the block who refused to try the fruit was Mr. Sun, Pang Ayi's husband. A retired railway inspector, he had a stubborn streak and refused to eat most fruits, preferring instead to subsist on his wife's hand-pulled noodles and crescent-moon-shaped dumplings. He was a sober man, not given to talking much, though he did inveigh against the *qiguo* when his wife asked. "Not natural," he said. "Don't trust it. Sunshan, pah!"

The founder of Sunshan Produce, Fan Shiyi, was feted everywhere that season. He was a tiny, wizened old man, usually pictured on television standing before a grove laden with the *qiguo.*

The trees were short, their branches gnarled, the fruit glowing red and orange against their deeply dark leaves. Often his wife was pictured with him, grinning, gap-toothed, at the camera.

By the end of that spring, we all knew Fan Shiyi's story by heart: how the old man had crossbred fruit as a hobby for years, how so many of his experiments had tasted sour or mealy or had withered on the vine before he had finally invented the *qiguo*—healthy, full of vitamins, and delicious!

The state media embraced Fan Shiyi's tale of success. The *qiguo* was a symbol of grassroots ingenuity, its reporters said, "a new fruit that is a symbol of our new nation."

We ate it standing by the sink, juices running down our chins. We ate it in smoothies while strolling and sliced atop frozen yogurt. In classrooms, teachers handed it out to students; it was said it made the brightest pupils more clever, the recalcitrant ones more heedful of their classmates' needs. In our neighborhood, on our block, those of us who ate it found the sun seemed to shine with an unwonted brightness, the tree leaves reflecting a more brilliant shade of jade. Even the surly *bao'an,* the man who guarded the front gate, began smiling and nodding at residents who came and went.

The season, though, didn't last. The last trucks bearing *qiguo* arrived in late May, and by early summer, the fruit was no longer being sold. Instead we roamed the supermarket aisles discontentedly, passing piles of pears and apricots and bananas, which now tasted insipid and wooden, without flavor. We bought more of the fruits that reminded us of the *qiguo*—nectarines, oranges—and discarded them half-eaten.

Summer was unusually hot that year. As the weeks went by, we grew increasingly irritable with one another, prickly with the heat. Couples fought. The noise of children chasing one another in the courtyard grated on our nerves. Without the *qiguo,* babies fussed in the humidity and refused their mothers' breasts. A few blocks away, the No. 8 Production Facility workers went on strike after one of their number succumbed to heat and overwork and died; the girl had been just sixteen years old.

Pang Ayi, though, remained in good temper. In fact she had blossomed astoundingly. Before, we had thought of her as little more than the neighborhood gossip, a woman who had borne two children and excelled at dumpling-making and, yes, resembled to a certain degree a dumpling herself, who usually wore the same cheap full-legged slacks and a baggy, gauzy shirt. That summer, though, we noticed that she had gotten a perm and had taken to wearing short, flouncy skirts in bright colors, the kind other women would go dancing in. She had been observed snapping a half-opened rose off one of the bushes that grew in the apartment's courtyard and putting it, absurdly, in her hair.

Often she and Lao Zhou could now be found chatting in the market, lingering over the cauliflower and long beans. On several afternoons, she and the widower were seen climbing a jasmine-covered hill at a nearby park and lunching on some of her crescent-moon-shaped dumplings while gazing at the view.

Some of us remembered that when Pang Ayi's youngest son had broken his leg all those years ago and Mr. Sun was away traveling, it was Lao Zhou who had carried him to find a rickshaw. "He's always been devoted to her," we told one another.

Summer mellowed into fall, and the heat finally broke. Carina Wei's new hit, "My Sweet Qiguo," was released, and for a few months, the treacly single played everywhere, on buses and in supermarkets. It was a love song: *From the bitter comes the sweet, my baby, my sweet strange fruit.* When the song came on, a peculiar feeling would steal over the crowd: a kind of backward yearning. Often someone would begin to hum, and soon more than a few of us would be singing. With so many voices, it was curious; the cloying lyrics took on the feeling of something more like a dirge.

Winter came, and with it the same dry chapped skin, the same routine of heavy cabbage-and-leek dishes, two vegetables that we stockpiled in the courtyard. Our troubles weighed more heavily on us, somehow, that season. The city looked more colorless, the gray sky pinning us in. We thought of the family we had lost; our sleep was burdened with too many dreams. On one especially cold night, the old woman who lived on the fourth floor burned some coal without first opening her exhaust vents; she suffocated on the carbon monoxide and died. It was an accident, we said.

All of us looked forward to the spring, and a new season of fruit.

This time the *qiguo* were sold exclusively to supermarket chains —you couldn't buy them from street peddlers anymore. They were wrapped differently, too, each piece surrounded by a collar of green foam and swathed in white tissue paper, sold by the dozen in a decorative box. The cost had gone up accordingly, and, naturally, we groused.

But it didn't matter, not much, so eager were we to taste the fruit again, to hold it in our hands and again be moved by the feelings that it conjured. On the first day it arrived on shelves, we lined up outside the supermarket for more than an hour with our neighbors, an air of festivity beckoning. Some shops, we heard, were rationing it: only two boxes per buyer. We smiled at one another, we greeted one another, we basked in the springlike weather.

"At last," we told one another. "At last."

As we waited, we swapped our stories. Zhu Ayi said that her wheelchair-bound mother had been indoors for years before trying the *qiguo,* which imparted a wonderful scent of flowers that finally tempted her outside to the courtyard. "Now she goes outside every day," she said.

"The first one I ate made me feel like I was twenty-five again," Mr. Feng was heard to say loudly, toward the back of the line. It was clear that he'd tried to capture the same look, too, had taken to combing the remains of his hair over his bald pate, and ever since the previous spring had been regularly spotted doing energetic calisthenics out in the courtyard.

But the next morning, we dodged one another's eyes uncomfortably; we stared at our feet.

We had gone hurriedly home with our parcels, had unwrapped the fruit and washed it with ceremony. The *qiguo* tasted the same, the rich texture and resistant flesh that our teeth sank slowly through, the sweetness, with its notes of acid beneath. This time, though, the feelings that followed were dark and discordant, the emotional equivalent of a stomachache.

Alone at home in his kitchen, Mr. Feng had cut expectantly into the fruit. After consuming a few tart pieces, though, he'd begun coughing and had to sit down, a feeling of bile rising up in him as he remembered the look of the old man in a dunce cap that he and some of his schoolmates had beaten until he'd collapsed and . . . well . . . it was many years ago and those were different times. Nonetheless, he buried his head in his arms and it took ten minutes before the wave of nausea receded.

The phone rang several times before he picked it up. It was a friend whom he'd seen in line earlier that day. "Was it good?" his friend asked.

"Very good," Mr. Feng had said, after a pause. "How about yours?"

"Excellent."

We were lying to one another, covering up the fruit's effects. Zhu Ayi, when she'd eaten her first piece, was swept with a feeling of shame so powerful that for a moment her vision blurred. There was the time she'd left her son alone and he'd scalded himself on the stove, the time she'd fed her mother-in-law a piece of fish that had fallen on the floor—these and other memories, surging up and reproaching her.

Inside his home, Lao Zhou finished a plate of *qiguo* and was immediately flooded with a grief so vast and unfathomable that he sat stunned. When he closed his eyes, all he could picture was a man who was forced to wear a big sign about his neck that read BOUR-GEOISIE, kneeling before a crowd. The man was his father, a calligrapher. He did not see him again until he was buried, days after being stoned. Lao Zhou sat at his table without moving, and for two days after that, he didn't go outside.

Occasionally a piece of fruit would restore to us a memory of that first *qiguo* season, a skipping of the heart, like being swung out by a dance partner; a warm feeling of contentment, like being surrounded by one's family, well and whole and happy. Most of the time, though, the fruit carried with it feelings of remorse, and shame.

And yet we kept eating it. Not so often, of course. But you could hope for a good piece, and anyway we craved its flavor, which lingered for a few glorious moments before the dark feelings began to set in.

Soon, newspaper headlines were reporting what we already knew. It was a bad season, they said, a bad season.

Some of us tried pickling the *qiguo,* or fermenting it. We tried cooking it, adding sugar and mixing it in a compote with other fruits. None of it improved its effects. Before long, supermarkets were running sales: PECULIAR FRUIT, HALF-PRICE.

We wanted answers. On television, when he was interviewed, Fan Shiyi of Sunshan Produce said that there had been unusually heavy rain that season, creating high levels of acidity in the soil, which might explain any irregularities. "It should be ripened properly before being eaten," he said, but his words didn't carry much conviction, we felt. His wife had stopped appearing on camera.

Nationwide, odd stories had begun to surface. There was a middle-school student whose mother had packed a *qiguo* in his lunch; the boy had climbed up to the school's roof that afternoon and jumped. There was a businessman who abruptly announced he was giving away half his fortune, and in interviews was frequently seen dabbing at his eyes; we assumed he had eaten a *qiguo* and was trying to atone for some guilty past.

In our neighborhood, it was Pang Ayi who changed the most. You saw the change in the pinched expression on her face, in the way her permed hair had gone frizzy, in the distant, almost embarrassed look she had in her eyes. Now, when other women ran into her in the common privy, instead of companionably chatting as they squatted side by side, Pang Ayi would hastily finish up and leave.

All her life, Pang Ayi had been a supremely practical woman. She had married Mr. Sun, a man with a steady job at the railway bureau; she'd put up with his long absences. She had borne two children and worked for thirty-four years at a textile mill before retiring with a modest pension. She and Mr. Sun did not share many passions, but what was passion? They were sixty-three years old. Mr. Sun was a steady worker who did not mind her chatter. He liked her cooking, and she enjoyed cooking for him. They were fond of each other, and that was more than you could say about most marriages.

And yet, she couldn't deny she had formed an attachment as of late to Lao Zhou. The two of them saw eye to eye, she thought. What other people saw as a gossip's instinct was really a fierce desire simply to *notice* things, to see the *possibilities* in things and what they meant, whether it was a certain expression that flitted across a neighbor's face or a flock of starlings on the roof. Lao Zhou was the same way, she thought. He noticed everything about her.

Still, all through that previous year, Pang Ayi had been convinced there was no reason to speak to her husband about the matter. She did not want to leave him, did not want to hurt him. It was enough, she thought, simply to see Lao Zhou in the market, to bring to him occasional helpings of her crescent-moon-shaped dumplings, to walk with each other in the cool of the evening and feel the embers of an old friendship gently stirred. Occasionally she felt his hand at her elbow. Once in the darkness he had slipped his arm about her waist and they had walked like that for half a block.

But that spring, halfway through the *qiguo* box she had bought at the supermarket, Pang Ayi felt a sense of shame surge within her, so powerful that she gripped the counter to steady herself. At the time she had been standing in the kitchen, cutting jewel-colored slices of the fruit and placing them in her mouth. By the time she finished the rest of the *qiguo,* tart and delicious, she abhorred herself, so much so that she deliberately took the kitchen knife and let it waver in the air for a moment before jerkily throwing it across the counter, away from her. Then she sat down on the floor, crying.

When Mr. Sun came in at the sound of the clatter and asked her what was wrong, she told him.

A few short minutes later, the rest of us saw Mr. Sun descend from his apartment and blindly walk across the courtyard. He wore an old felt hat, inappropriate for the season. He looked like a man who had received a sudden, swift blow and did not know what to do with himself. He ignored our greetings and walked stiffly out of the compound and in a straight line for a half-block before he crossed the street against the light and was struck by a speeding motorcycle.

He lay motionless in the gutter, as our voices rose around him in an urgent clamor.

For the rest of us, life went on.

We no longer blanched when a husband or wife or child dissolved into silent tears and had to leave the dining table. We grew accustomed to the fact that on some days, certain shops simply did not open, their owners lying in bed, wracked with grief or guilt.

Gradually we learned the topography of one another's sorrows. Zhu Ayi told us that her first child had been stillborn; twenty years later, she was still mourning it, she said as she brokenly sorted through a pile of bruised tomatoes at the market. The *bao'an* confessed that he'd gotten into a drunken fight one night and left a man bleeding and facedown by the side of the road; he wasn't sure what had happened to him.

Lao Zhou did not need to speak for us to know what he was feeling. He loitered often in the courtyard, waiting for Pang Ayi to come home. He avoided our eyes in the market and went home carrying solitary bags of parsnips and dandelion greens. He had taken up the *guzheng,* which we heard him playing into the night, terribly, with out-of-tune strings.

After her husband had been struck by the motorcycle, Pang Ayi kept vigil in the hospital for days. His lungs were bruised; he had fractured three ribs and now lay in a thick cast. He had an air of bewilderment about him and periodically stole looks at his wife, who, after her first apology, whispered as he'd been wheeled into the emergency room, had sat quietly in a metal folding chair opposite his bed and mostly stared out the window.

He did not know what would happen between them. But every day he kept waking up, and she was still there. She brought him soup made of pigs' bones and stuffed buns that she shaped and steamed at home herself. Occasionally she sat peeling apples without meeting his eyes. On the third day, he ate some as a concession to her.

One day in that season of fruit, a graying man we did not recognize wandered into our compound to look for a retired professor, Lao Song, who lived on the second floor. Lao Song was sitting out in the courtyard at the time; his rheumatism was again acting up—we could tell by the way he occasionally shook out his right knee. Together, we watched as the stranger approached and knelt before him. "Three days before your father killed himself, I was among those who whipped him and spit on him and called him a capitalist pig," the man said, and began weeping. "I was young then, I am old now, I am sorry."

The same tableaus, we heard, were happening across the country, breaking a decades-old taboo. Sometimes they ended badly; many could not forgive. But it was not unusual, either, to see old men and women in the street with tears in their eyes, embracing or eating pieces of the *qiguo* as they traded recollections: the mother whose hair had gone white overnight, the belts we had used on our victims, the temples we had defiled.

Not long after that, we celebrated the day of the martyrs. It was a day of televised spectacle: Carina Wei sang "My Sweet Qiguo" on the noon broadcast, and dance groups and singers all over put on performances. The day culminated with the nation's leaders paying a state visit to the martyrs' monument, clad in somber black suits and bowing before the white marble, flanked by elaborate floral sculptures. Each leader made a speech in turn, the same statements that we knew by heart—the price we'd paid for our great new nation, the ultimate worth of what we'd accomplished, the bright future that we shared.

The final man to take the podium was older than the rest; we could see it cost him some effort to mount the stairs. He turned to gaze at the martyrs' monument behind him, a solid white slab like a tomb. The wind whipped the remaining strands of his hair. Then, all of us watching saw his face suddenly crumple, and tears began to squeeze their way out of his eyes and travel down the corrugated wrinkles of his face. "I'm sorry," he gasped, and for a moment his rheumy eyes stared straight ahead into the camera. "I'm sorry," he said again, and then the feed abruptly went to black.

The government banned the *qiguo* the next day. The fruit disappeared off the shelves nearly overnight, the signs PECULIAR FRUIT, HALF-PRICE replaced with PEACHES: EXTRA SWEET and a special deal on roasted nuts. Those of us who went to the supermarket looking for the *qiguo* wandered the aisles part in sorrow, part in relief.

Not long afterward, word spread that the Sunshan farm had been cordoned off with barbed wire and was surrounded twenty-four hours a day by an armed guard. Later, we heard, the government set the entire *qiguo* grove ablaze. The tiny, wizened Fan Shiyi and his gap-toothed wife disappeared; no one knew what had become of them.

Weeks passed, and soon it was summer. Watermelon vendors appeared with their street carts, hawking freshly sliced pink shards tipped with green rinds on sticks. The summer was even hotter than the year before, and we ate piles of watermelon to stave off the heat, even though, to most of us, its flesh had lost its flavor. We ate it crushed with ice, we ate it sticky-fingered with our children in the courtyard, we ate it sitting out in the sun until our heads ached.

In the months after Mr. Sun left the hospital, Pang Ayi regained some of her old aplomb. She stopped wearing flouncy skirts, was again clad in the same slippers and baggy gauze shirts that were perpetually on sale in the markets. When we encountered her outside, her appetite for companionable gossip seemed to be returning. She noticed the *bao'an* poring over books late at night; she'd seen the titles and suspected he was going to try to qualify as a policeman. She noted the fourth-floor apartment once inhabited by the woman who'd died of carbon monoxide poisoning was being renovated; probably the family was planning to sell.

Lao Zhou no longer came to the neighborhood market. Occasionally we saw him bicycling in the morning in the opposite direction, toward a different market where we presumed he now bought his fruits and vegetables. When he and Pang Ayi passed each other in the street, we all held our breath, but they simply nodded at each other without evident emotion. At night we still heard him playing the *guzheng;* he was getting better.

Most of us have heard by now that the government is supposedly developing a new variety of the *qiguo,* superior in flavor, more stable in its effects. They say it will be sweeter, that its trees will bear fruit in all seasons. Especially as the winter sets in, we are impatient to try it.

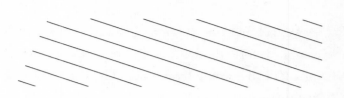

FIELD NOTES ON
A MARRIAGE

IT WAS NOT A PLACE, GAO SAID, THAT HE WANTED TO GO. "It's not a very nice country," he said. "Dirty, but without being charming." We had only two weeks and we should spend it someplace romantic, a real honeymoon destination, he said. I protested. As a child my favorite doll had been a Chinese porcelain girl with stiff black plaits and gold-veined red pajamas, and tiny satin booties that matched. I'd always wanted to go. "I'd like to see where you're from," I told him, but he shook his head: another time.

We had met that previous October. I must have seen him on campus before, though I don't know that I would have noticed him. If I had, I would have thought he was a graduate student. He had that look, somewhat underfed, and habitually wore a leather coat that I would later tease him about, zipped tightly around his middle. It made him look like an aspiring motorcycle rider instead of what he was, a newly minted associate professor of German with a few promising publications under his belt.

The coffee shop where I usually did my work was crowded that day. He arrived and looked inquiringly at the seat beside me, and I smiled and pushed aside the anthropology syllabus I was working on. I noted the book he was reading, a Pushkin biography, and we got to talking. Gao had a funny demeanor that took a while to parse: restrained, almost haughty at first, but sometimes he'd break out in a hearty bout of laughter that took you by surprise. He was very entertained, for example, by the fact that I'd grown up on a farm.

"A farm!" he said, and burst out laughing. "No, really. Goats, cows, that kind of thing?"

"Alfalfa, actually," I said, smiling. "Indiana." I couldn't tell what he found so amusing, but he was so pleased I found myself laughing as well.

As I later learned, the stop-off for coffee was part of his post-gym routine, prior to heading back to his office. He was, in all things, rigidly disciplined. He spent two hours a day at the gym working through a precise program he'd designed himself, quadriceps and laterals, a routine that sounded to me like a series of math problems. Then he'd head home and eat a half-pound of Brussels

sprouts, boiled from a bag on the stove. He never touched anything with sugar, or anything fried. "I'm not interested in food,"
he told me.

At first it was a walk in a botanical garden, lunch at a brightly
lit café, a visit to a weekend flea market. I had almost reconciled
myself to thinking we were simply friends when, during a student
chamber-music concert one evening, Gao slipped his hand over
mine. Afterward, standing on the sidewalk, we exchanged some
chaste, dry-lipped kisses, hands fumbling experimentally about
each other as though we were teenagers.

He didn't like to talk about himself, something that I found refreshing, almost old-fashioned after so many years spent in a con-
fessional university environment. "You're from China," I said on
our second meeting as we strolled amid the spiked leaves of the botanical garden, a section devoted to North American desert plants.
I looked at him expectantly, and he nodded, as though this were
part of a series of formalities he had to endure. "Where in China?"

"Someplace you've never heard of," he said, and named it. "It's
a backwater."

"Rickshaws and rice paddies?" I joked, and he shrugged. "You
could say that." I asked him how he'd learned German, but there,
too, he was laconic, saying only that he'd gotten a high school
scholarship to go to Europe, and that he'd stayed. "I haven't been
back since I was sixteen," he said indifferently, meaning home, in a
tone that discouraged questions.

He wanted to know all about me, though, to hear about my
fieldwork, my family; he had a greediness for knowledge of me that
I'd never experienced before, at once intoxicating and intensely

flattering. He wanted to know everything from childhood nicknames to details of my school science fairs, studying me as intently as if he might have to someday defend our relationship to a panel of colleagues.

"You're so self-sufficient," Gao said to me, early in our courtship. It was after he'd visited my apartment for the first time and opened the refrigerator to see the rows of Tupperware neatly stacked, the shopping list registered in a precise hand. He'd meant it as a compliment, and after a pause, I thanked him.

One Saturday six weeks later we spent the afternoon in my bedroom, naked in the bright sunlight, inspecting each other curiously, without desire, as though we were museum curators cataloging idiosyncrasies: the raised mole here, a pale depression of stretch marks there. The afternoon light came in through the window, irradiating every body hair. I felt lazy, warm, and speculative. We'd been half watching a Spanish soap opera, me periodically offering up translations; the plot (involving a marriage ceremony in which the priest removed a false beard and revealed himself to be the bride's lover) kept us laughing.

"You've never done it, right?" he said, when we turned the TV off. "Gotten married."

"No," I said, staring at the ceiling. It hadn't bothered me. There were a lot of things I hadn't done: run a marathon, become a doctor, developed a taste for Mediterranean food. There were a lot of things I had.

"Why don't we?" Gao said.

"You're joking."

"Why not?" he said. I turned over then, and looked at him. He was lying with his head propped up on one arm, gazing at me with an unreadable expression.

"We hardly know each other."

"I'm serious. We get along, don't we?"

I flopped back onto the bed, astonished. "Okay," I said, feeling small flickers of happiness start to curl inside me. "Let's do it."

He rolled over on top of me and tickled the underside of my chin with his finger. "You're sure, *häschen*?" he said. It meant "bunny," an animal I never liked — too anxious, too red-eyed — but I didn't mind the endearment when he used it.

I nodded. "Okay," he said, and rose, humming. "What are you doing tomorrow, then?" I reached out, laughing, trying to pull him back down, but he went to the kitchen, where I heard the tap being turned on and the sound of ice being cracked and water running. Even after living in the U.S. for more than a decade, Gao still couldn't get over the fact that he could drink from the tap, could drink a dozen glasses a day.

After we married, Gao's relentless questions about me stopped, as though I were a topic that his restless brain had sufficiently mastered. We folded ourselves into each other's lives neatly, seamlessly. He moved into my apartment with just two suitcases' worth of clothes; all his books and papers lived at his office. Our dish rack held two plates and two mugs, mine maroon and his green, that we rinsed and replaced every night.

We went to Indiana for a week to see my parents, where Gao shucked corn from the market with my mom and rode a tractor on the farm with my dad. At night we sat with the porch door open and listened to the crickets in the grass. Usually I grew antsy there, felt stranded, but I could see that something about the life appealed to Gao. He was the ideal guest, eating things he wouldn't usually touch—bacon, thick pancakes—and asked my parents dozens of questions about the farm in a way that reminded me of how he'd been when we'd first met. They responded as I had: flattered, instantly wooed. (They also asked me if he was a Chinese spy: "He's so fit!" my mother said, and looked almost disappointed when I said no.)

"Actually, Gao grew up on a farm, too," I told them over breakfast on our second day.

"No kidding!" my dad said.

I saw Gao hesitate. "Not really," he said.

"I thought you said you grew up in the countryside?"

"More like a small town," he said. "My mom was a high school principal," he added. "My dad was a government official."

I hadn't known either of these things, and it made me feel foolish, exposed. I got up, annoyed, and went out to the porch with a glass in hand, expecting him to follow, but he didn't, and after a few minutes I returned, not wanting to make a scene.

In the months after that, Gao was often away, working late at the office or spending hours at the gym. I didn't mind; I still hadn't accustomed myself to spending so much time with another person. Though we took many of our weekday meals apart, we ate dinner together at a Sichuan restaurant every Friday, dining on petal-soft pieces of white fish cooked with blood-red chilies that made my lips tingle.

Now and then we'd go for a hike along the fire trails up in the hills. We were good companions. Only occasionally did it occur to me to wish for something more. For our first anniversary — paper — he'd given me a beautifully fashioned set of origami boxes that he'd made himself. I'd opened them, expecting a gift inside, and flushed when I found them empty, realizing my mistake, hoping he hadn't noticed.

At night these memories swim up to me, unbidden. Most of the time I pat them on the head and send them away, releasing them back into dark waters. I tell myself it doesn't do to fixate too much on the dead: apart from everything else, they can't answer you.

The journey to Gao's hometown was six thousand miles and seventeen hours. Flight attendants came through the aisles offering tea and almond cookies. I leaned my forehead against the inky, cold window and watched the plane icon trace our passage on the blue and green map on the screen before me. As we neared our destination, the airline played a welcome video of misty pagodas and a pond flecked with golden fish, observed by a woman dressed in trailing magenta robes and carrying a paper parasol.

The scene outside the airport nearest Gao's hometown was considerably less appealing: sprawling lines of warehouses that ran for miles in bleak repetition, hardly the small town Gao had described, though I supposed it might still have been one when he left. As we entered its outskirts, I felt the cabdriver eyeing me, a woman alone in his backseat. "America," he said. It wasn't a question. "Yes," I said, in an attitude of brightness, but he just nodded.

After an hour, we reached the hotel, a stained concrete block adorned with a sign that read GOLD PHOENIX VILLA. Tinny advertisements blared from a shop selling hosiery across the street.

Inside, the hotel's lobby was cold and featured a faded watch ad depicting a Western couple. The woman had sallow cheeks and a wide nose that wouldn't have made the cut in an American advertisement, posing beside a blond man who smiled with the grimace of a serial killer appearing in a family portrait.

Gao's mother met me there the next morning. She wore her hair in tightly wound curls and had on a purple velour tracksuit, and came straight over and took my arm with a warmth that I didn't expect. Neither she nor Gao's father had come to his funeral, and I had tried not to judge them for it, unsuccessfully.

"You're here," she said, and briskly steered me outside, not quite making eye contact. "Welcome."

"I'm so pleased to meet you," I said, a little self-consciously. "I've wanted to come here for so long."

Outside in the parking lot, she slid her legs behind the wheel of a dark-gray sedan and made an elaborate performance of adjusting the mirrors. "My baby, new," she said, and laughed, as though to make sure I knew it was a joke. She had studied English in college, Gao had told me, but even so, her apparent ease with the language surprised me.

We drove for a while, passing shops with drab pasteboard signs I couldn't read, though some gave clues to their wares: a picture of tools and nails, another of a sheep standing before a pot (presumably a restaurant of some sort). All around us, rain darkened the road.

She had not invited me to visit; I had invited myself, and as we drove in silence, I wondered if I was truly welcome. "It's good to be here," I finally said, tentatively. "Gao told me so much about this place."

It wasn't true, and perhaps she sensed it, simply nodding. There was a temple, she said, she'd take me. There was a museum, as well, not very large. What else did I want to see?

"Anything from Gao's childhood," I said.

She said there wasn't much left: The government had torn down their old family home years ago and replaced it with a shopping mall. The school had been converted into government offices.

I was sorry, but tried not to show it. "I'd still like to see it," I said.

"The mall?" The fact that Gao's mother had been a high school principal showed, I thought; beyond the perm and purple velour, she had an aura of steely competence to her.

I said yes, but she shook her head impatiently. "There's nothing there. You should see some history. This city has four thousand years of history."

When I agreed, she smiled and turned on the radio, drowning out the need for further conversation.

Gao hadn't been a popular child, he told me, but he'd commanded a certain amount of respect because of his mother's position. Other parents, in particular, fawned over him. They passed him sweets when picking up their children after school, they praised his cleverness. Eventually he drew to him a small coterie of boys like himself, bright and a little insecure. Their names regularly topped the list of students with the best grades, posted weekly outside the school gates for all the parents to see.

But there was one boy who always outdid everyone in both reading and math, not of their group, whom they called Mouse. He was one of the boarders, had come from a village a day's travel away. Gao shrugged when I'd asked about the nickname. "He was small," he said.

As the high school entrance exam neared, students studied six days a week, eleven hours a day, and Gao hardest of all, because everyone expected him to do well. "You can't imagine what the pressure was like," he told me. "It was cruel."

At the time, we were in Germany on our honeymoon and he'd taken me to see the university where he'd done his degree. We'd visited the carrel in the library where he used to study and the classroom where he'd defended his dissertation, and it was there that he'd paused, and for a while it didn't seem like he'd ever want to move again. "So you can imagine how glad I was to get away," he said.

At the temple, I asked Gao's mother what her son was like as a child. "He was a good student," she said. We were standing side by side, staring at a statue of a robed god painted blue, with vermillion eyes. She had linked her arm firmly through mine, making it hard to see her expression, though when I asked her what else she could remember, I could feel her sigh at my side, just a little.

"He was very well behaved. Hardworking, good at his studies."

Something about her repetition of these qualities annoyed me, and I walked away on the pretext of examining a placard more closely. "Was he a happy kid?" I asked.

"Yes, of course," she said, voice defensive.

"It's a shame he never came back," I said.

"Not really. Why should he?"

We resumed walking. The temple was composed of a series of courtyards, with one long corridor dotted with small niches containing scores of Buddhas cast in shiny gold plastic. The green and white and maroon stripes swirled about the ceiling's wooden beams looked freshly painted, and there were heaps of new tiles and nails scattered about. A sign said that the temple had been destroyed in a fifteenth-century fire and rebuilt, and damaged in an earthquake and rebuilt again.

"It has a history of six hundred years," Gao's mother said. "Very old. Not like your America."

We walked farther, and she urged me to stand in front of a Buddha statue, and snapped a photo of me with my camera. Already that afternoon she'd had me pose before an inscribed stele, a rock formation, and a small pavilion. My cheeks hurt from smiling.

"How about over there?" she asked, gesturing to another courtyard. I went over, not wanting to disappoint her. She took another photo, one I didn't smile for. Finally, to my relief, we began moving toward the exit.

"Would Gao ever have come here?" I asked.

She thought about it, then shook her head. "It's mostly for tourists."

"Well," I said, and didn't have anything else to add. "It's very pretty," I said flatly.

After two years of marriage, Gao seemed to draw still further into himself. He spent increasingly long hours at the office, but his publications were sparse and failed to gain attention; he'd recently been passed over for a grant that he once would have won easily. The German department wasn't large and that semester had hired a young Ukrainian scholar fresh from his Ph.D. whom everyone considered its next star. One day I came into Gao's office and found him with his head in his arms. I stood there for a few minutes, watching him, before touching him on the shoulder. He said he'd been sleeping.

We were celebrating our second anniversary when Gao told me the rest of Mouse's story. We'd gone to the Sichuan restaurant downtown, where the maître d' had given us a table beside the big plate-glass window. The waiter brought us fish, rice, and cubes of tofu cooked with chilies, bristling with dashes of green onion. A cluster of unopened chrysanthemums sat between us, curled like tiny fists in a small vase. It had been a long day for Gao at the office, a department meeting and hours spent revising a paper that had already been rejected twice for publication, and he was quiet. The restaurant was quiet, too — it was a weeknight — and I wondered if the waiters could tell there was something wrong. Outside, it had grown dark, and I imagined that we looked like a pair of silent actors to passersby on the sidewalk, seen through the lit window as though onstage.

"Tell me something," I said to him, when the silence had gone on too long.

"Like what?"

"Anything. Something I don't know about you."

"You first," he said. With a fork, he began to carefully debone the fish, extracting each wispy fragment with his fingertips.

"Okay," I said. "Are you sure you don't want to order some wine?" He nodded and placed his hand over mine. It was a gesture I'd noticed he'd been using more and more; lately it had stopped feeling affectionate and more like someone gently closing your mouth.

I told him the story of our first cat. She was supposed to be mine, but she never liked me much, always preferred my parents' bed. I used to sneak into my parents' room to snatch her and make her sleep with me, I told him, only to wake to hear her scratching at the door, trying to get out. "She died when I was in college," I told him, attempting a laugh. "Up until the end, she didn't like me very much."

He smiled absently and wiped his mouth. "Stupid cat."

"Your turn," I said. He protested he had nothing to share, but I pressed him. Finally he folded his napkin and put it on the table and a strange look came over his face. "I'll tell you something," he said slowly, "since you ask."

He told me that when he and his friends turned fourteen, somehow it was decided among them that Mouse was a Japanese spy. He'd come from far away; no one knew his antecedents. He looked odd, with hair that was paler than that of the rest. ("I know now it was probably malnutrition," Gao said.) He was unbeatable in tests, "almost militaristic," they told one another. He had a funny white shirt they became convinced was cut in a Japanese style.

For months, they watched him closely for clues. Someone had seen him make a nighttime trip to the bathroom; it was possible he was meeting secret accomplices. A teacher had kept him after class; perhaps the two were in league. At some point he went back to his village. It was said his grandmother had died, but Gao and his friends knew better: Mouse was training in the hills. When he came back, it was as though all their fears were confirmed. The attack he was training for would come any day now, they said.

Gradually their plot took shape. "It was a game at first," Gao said. He stole some rat poison from the janitor. "We joked it was rat poison for a mouse," he said. Another boy, not to be outdone, befriended Mouse, started eating lunch with him. A third obtained still more rat poison in case the first attempt failed. It was the second boy who slipped a generous dose of it into Mouse's stir-fried eggplant at the canteen.

"Oh, God," I said. "What happened?"

Gao looked at me as though I'd asked a stupid question. "He died, of course," he said with irritation.

I didn't know what to say. "Did they ever catch anyone?"

He didn't answer me for a while. "One boy," he said eventually. "The boy who gave him the poison."

When the boy's parents came from their home village in the mountains to take the body away, the mother hysterical, the father wooden and stunned, they realized their mistake: Mouse's parents were poor villagers, speaking in a tongue so heavy and coarse the school administrators had trouble understanding them.

"And then you went to Germany," I said.

He nodded. "And then I went to Germany."

That spring, when the rains came, the ants invaded our apartment, making wobbly black lines across the bathroom. We bought a tub of petroleum and erected walls of it across the linoleum to try and stop their steady march. When that failed, Gao stood guard with the hose of a vacuum cleaner at the ready, determined to catch any escapees. The morning-glory vines that clung to our front porch unfurled themselves in purple trumpets. He seemed more relaxed after our conversation, I thought. He laughed more frequently, and spent more time at home. We started talking about having a family. We were going to begin trying any day now.

Then came a night when I'd fallen asleep over a stack of student papers and awoke just after dawn. Gao had said he'd be back after a late bout of grading at his office, but his side of the bed was undisturbed, the apartment empty. I made myself some coffee, called his office, paced impatiently for a while, and finally went to the car.

The morning chill was still in the air, the kind of cold that makes you expect birdsong. Gao's building was locked. I rapped on his window, but there was no reply. I found the facilities management office and waited until it opened. A janitor accompanied me back and unlocked the door: Gao's chair was pushed tidily in, the place empty. I flicked on the light anyway, futilely. "Thanks," I said, smiling, trying not to appear alarmed. "He must have lost track of time somewhere—I'll check the library."

He wasn't there. I tried the gym, searching through rows of undergraduates, with their ellipticals, neat ponytails, and elastic skin, but Gao wasn't among them. I stopped at the café where we'd first met, where the owner was just unlocking the doors, bleary-eyed. Finally I circled back to our home—maybe he'd returned in my absence.

He hadn't. I made myself more coffee and sat on the couch. I put a blanket on. I thought perhaps he was angry with me, I scoured my mind to try and remember any unintended slight. I sat there all day, reheating bowls of soup, until the phone rang at 4 p.m. It was the local police, called in by the parks department. They'd found him.

It was an elderly man out walking his border collie in the hills who'd made the report. Gao's body was dangling from a tree, face black, clad in his leather jacket, ID and car keys in his breast pocket. He'd been there all night. His car had been found in the otherwise empty parking lot, an index card with my name and number written in his hand on the dashboard. I searched the apartment in disbelief for days, but there wasn't anything else, no apology, no note of explanation. He had been private in almost everything, and he was private, too, in his death.

The days proceeded in his absence: phone calls with friends and funeral homes, details that needed arranging. Friends waited for confidences, but I was numb, I had none to share. Our marriage had been brief, I said. I was sorry it was over. His life had been his own, I told myself, to do with it what he would, and he did.

After the funeral, though, that sentiment cracked, and a chasm opened up within me. At night I buried myself under a pile of his shirts as I lay in bed, imagining the child we might have had together (his cheeks, my eyes). I found myself crying in grocery aisles and at the lecture podium, tears that came on quickly and tapered with equal speed. I resigned myself to their appearance; it was like a new cardiac rhythm or myopia, something unfamiliar but irrevocably now a part of me.

I kept his mug and plate in the dish rack. I kept a pair of his loafers by the front door. I began to feel an unreasonable resentment toward those whose marriages had been ruptured by affairs or neglect or abandonment, for their clarity of answers, or the fact that they could pick up the phone, at least, and demand them.

Whole weeks would go by and I couldn't remember what had happened in them.

Fall passed, and then winter. When I looked up from my desk it was spring, and the dean was standing in the doorway. A leave of absence might be a good idea, she said. I had missed three of my classes in the past month, and students were complaining.

Not long after that, I found myself in the travel section of a bookshop and to my surprise—despite Gao's insistence on its remoteness—there it was, listed in a China guide: a brief entry on his hometown. It didn't sound very enticing, described as a "dingy stopover with good connection links and some adequate hotels," with two temples listed and one museum. But still it sent a jolt through me, to see it printed in black and white, a real place, with clearly listed directions on how to get there. A month later, when classes finished for the summer, I was on a plane.

After the museum—a crowded affair of jostling children competing to peer into Plexiglas boxes containing oxidized bronze and old coins—Gao's mother drove us silently back to their apartment on the town's outskirts, past the recently poured roads and new highrises dotting the landscape. Now and then we passed a few soon-to-be-demolished buildings that still showed signs of inhabitants: a line of laundry here, a toy tricycle there, a stooped man wandering with his hands behind his back.

Their apartment was a cramped two-bedroom on the eleventh floor, and as we entered, Gao's father shuffled to greet us in rubber slippers. He looked older than his wife and wore a soft-brimmed, flat black cap, and chuckled in greeting on seeing me. I liked him straightaway. "Hello," he said. He offered me some tiny candies wrapped in foil, chuckling some more; it appeared to be a tic of his.

"Ni hao," I quavered, and he beamed again.

"Please sit," Gao's mother said, and arranged me on the couch before heading to the kitchen. My legs ached, and I didn't protest. At the museum she had hovered by my side, reading the mangled English descriptions aloud to me as though I were a child, and if I missed a single display case, she would gesture me over to study its contents.

Gao's father sank into a chair beside me, looking pleased. The apartment had a transient look, nothing on the walls. I tried to speak with him, but he didn't understand me, and together instead we turned our attention to the television, where an androgynous host was interviewing a rail-thin woman who clutched a curly-haired dog to her chest.

"Are you sure I can't help?" I called to Gao's mother, craning my neck around the corner.

She stuck her head out from the doorway. "No need," she said. In one hand, she waved a slick-shelled gray shrimp at me, antennae twitching in a way that briefly made it look alive. "It's very easy."

From the kitchen, I could hear the pot sizzle, and when the androgynous interviewer's segment was over, I got up and followed the smell. Gao's mother was standing before a cutting board, mincing garlic into a sticky crumb, ginger into matchsticks. "That smells good," I said.

"There are some pictures in the other room," she said, without turning around. "You can have a look."

I left, feeling rebuffed. The study was strewn with books and papers in a way that seemed at odds with Gao's mother's clipped decisiveness. A stuffed orangutan sat on the desk, its tags still on. In one corner a dozen plants bulged from their pots, leaves filmed with dust. Beside them was a bookshelf adorned with framed photos. One showed a teenage Gao, slim as a fairy-tale waif, hair spiked with gel and wearing a white button-down open at the top. He looked young, and the sight of him made me catch my breath. Another showed him as a toddler, his parents crouched beside him and smiling as he extended his hand, as though it held something he wanted the photographer to see.

There was a noise behind me as Gao's mother entered the room, and I turned around, still holding the photo of him as a teenager. "That's Gao," I said, and managed a laugh.

"That's Gao in Germany," she said. It sounded like a correction.

I put the photo reluctantly back and thanked her for cooking. "I'm afraid I've given you a lot of trouble," I said insincerely.

"No trouble. Eat."

Gao's mother set the steamer of the once-gray shrimp, now turned rosy pink, in the center of a table in the living room, along with a dish of water chestnuts and pale cabbage. The three of us sat down, the television still on, fluorescent lights bright overhead.

The meal was strained. Gao's mother did not want to talk, replying only tersely when I asked her about the school, the neighborhood, the family. I kept trying to reach for answers anyway, feeling a mounting sense of frustration that after all my years of fieldwork, somehow in this most important of interviews, I could not seem to connect. The minutes ticked by. "Eat some more," she said brusquely, when I tried to ask her again about Gao's childhood. And then: "Why are you crying?"

I shook my head, embarrassed, and wiped my nose before returning to my chopsticks. When I looked up, though, she was still examining me. "I thought this trip would be different," I said at last, disliking the tremor in my voice.

"What did you think would be different?"

"Everything," I said. "I don't know."

A flicker of impatience crossed her face. She pulled napkins from their plastic holder and passed them to me.

"My son should never have gotten married," she said.

When I asked her what she meant, she appeared to consider saying something, then gave a little laugh. I couldn't tell whether she intended it for my benefit, and all at once I didn't care. "If you mean something, just say it," I said.

She ate steadily away, picking up another one of the shrimp, sliding it neatly from its skin and placing it in her mouth. Then she sighed and laid her chopsticks down.

"Gao was very competitive," she said. "But jealousy is no excuse for what they did to that poor boy."

I paused, not liking her version of the story. My hands felt suddenly very cold. "That's not what happened," I said slowly.

Gao's father said something to her, and she replied sharply. It occurred to me that theirs was not a happy marriage, or maybe it was just the shock of losing their son, far away in a country they'd never visited.

"I'm not going to sit here and listen to you attack him," I said. She lifted her glass but did not drink from it. She set it back down and looked at me, almost pityingly. "You didn't really know him."

Outside the light was fading as Gao's mother and I made our way back to the car. The cicadas thrummed noisily in the bushes around us. The sky was a faint pink, and the chill of the air felt good on my face.

"I'll get a cab," I said, but she said no. It felt like an overture until she explained: it wasn't an easy part of town to find one.

We drove along the highway, passing warehouses the size of city blocks and billboards with advertisements for new apartments and furniture stores. There was nothing remarkable about the scene, and I doubted Gao would have recognized any more of it than I did. Still, I took my camera and pointed it out the window anyway.

"Gao hated it here," his mother said abruptly. "I asked him to bring you, many times. He always said no."

We rounded along a curved overpass that flung us out onto a narrow road. On one side were low-slung shops and a gas station, and scattered cheap eateries on the other. We passed a few children riding their bikes along the side, yelling happily at one another, and soon a forest of closely packed apartment blocks reared up on our right. They looked new and mostly untenanted, windows that gaped without glass.

Farther along, the dense curtain of buildings parted, and as we neared the gap between them, I inhaled sharply.

"What is that?" I asked. "Can we stop?"

Gao's mother pulled over. Outside the passenger window, I could see the buildings had been erected atop landfill, but where they were interrupted, a cliff of earth fell away, and below that was a rocky wasteland strewn with debris and construction material. At its center stood a lone concrete house. At first glance the house looked as though it might be several floors high, until I realized the ground had been hollowed around it, scooped away from it like the base of a sculpture; the building stood atop stories of packed earth.

It looked like an odd art installation, or an image from a surrealist painting: a city melting into a puddle, a single house floating on its remains.

I asked if anyone actually lived there, and Gao's mother said yes. "It's called *dingzihu*," she explained. "The government wants to take their land but they won't move."

On the other hand, it seemed, whoever was inside couldn't leave the house, either. Apart from the difficulty in scaling down the rocky incline, she said, the developer would likely come and demolish the house if it was ever left empty.

"People bring them food," she said. "Look."

I got out, slamming the car door behind me, and she followed. We stood at the road's edge and watched a woman and a child pick their way across the rubble, holding a sheaf of bananas, a sleeve of crackers, and a big jug of bottled water. It took them a while. When they reached the house, we heard them shout up to the window. The window slid open, and a bucket tied to a rope was flung out.

From our vantage point, the woman and her child looked as

small as dolls. It was hard to see what happened next, but then the bucket was rising, slowly and jerkily pulled by an invisible hand.

"See? There's someone inside," Gao's mother said.

For a moment, I thought I saw a flash of a face at the window, but it disappeared too quickly to be sure. All I could see was the rope, and the bucket that hung from it, dangling.

We got back into the car. The light was fading, and we were two strangers anxious to get home.

FLYING MACHINE

IN THE AUTUMN OF HIS LIFE, AFTER THE CORN HAD RIPENED AND BEEN PLUCKED, CAO CAO DECIDED HE WOULD BUILD HIS OWN PLANE, THOUGH HE DID NOT KNOW HOW TO FLY.

He lived in a village of red brick and cement homes. He had a smiling face, as though someone had once told him a joke and he hadn't stopped laughing since. He had a great affection for his chickens, their tiny little heads and anxious, restless pecking. "Good morning, dummies," he would say cheerfully as he fed them.

One of his legs was shorter than the other, and though his wife folded wedges of fabric into his shoes, they weren't comfortable and he took them out. He was usually seen walking through the village at a jerky clip, sometimes to smoke and sit outside with his friend Old Li, or to the small shop at the village's entrance that sold chips and bottled drinks and domino-size packets of shampoo, a shop his wife swore he visited at least twice a day.

"It's too much," she'd say. "We are poor farmers, remember?"

Cao Cao did try to restrain himself, but then he would get thirsty and think of what a fine thing it would be to buy drinks or cigarettes for his friends as they sat and played cards. Or he was restless and wanted the clack of sunflower seeds under his teeth after a day spent in the field.

The idea that he was just a poor farmer, though — that was simply incorrect. In his bedroom was a stack of business cards that spoke of his true vocation. He'd had them printed up a decade ago, a stack of one hundred that had not dwindled noticeably since. INVENTOR AND GRASSROOTS ENGINEER, they read. Two years ago, when he had gotten a new phone number, he had gone back laboriously over them with a pen, correcting them.

What he really wanted to be was a party member. For fifteen years, he had submitted his application, copied out in duplicate by hand. *I am an ordinary farmer, but I truly feel that the Chinese Communist*

Party is the guide of our nation and its great revival, he wrote. *I solemnly apply to the party and strive to overcome my shortcomings and deficiencies, to try and become a glorious party member at an early date!* With it he attached his résumé, two lines written in careful blue ink: inventor, farmer, male, 68. Family background: farmer.

On each occasion, the village's party secretary, Jiang, a muskrat-faced man in a black windbreaker, rejected him kindly but firmly. All across the country, fortunes were being minted. The party wanted university students, not elderly farmers. It wanted brains, it wanted talent, it wanted (this was implied, but not spoken) wealth. Big Duck Village had just one other party member, a man who owned the village's sole thriving business, a company that pressed corn into corn oil. At the village's monthly meetings, he would sit with the party secretary, bent in conversation together at the back, like a parley of men among boys.

It stung, but Cao Cao wasn't one to dwell upon slights. When he was young, he had lived through a famine in which they ate the bark off trees! He'd seen the village since then electrified, paved with a road, reinforced with cement, grown noisy with motorcycles and mechanized tractors. He'd seen the village transform itself over a lifetime, just as he, too, was going to transform himself with an invention the likes of which his neighbors had never seen.

To that end, he had become a connoisseur of what others might call rubbish: rusted-through woks, old bicycle parts, broken farm implements. For years now, the villagers had made a habit of popping by Cao Cao's any time they had some unusual item they wanted to discard: a broken chair, leftover construction materials. The two little girls who lived next door had made it a private joke:

whenever they encountered something their parents made them put in the trash — a tiny scrap of soap, a discarded candy wrapper — they would giggle and say, "Give it to Cao Cao!"

Actually, Cao Cao would have found a use for both and not been offended in the bargain. The candy wrapper, for example, could be cut into a decorative flower for his robot's hat. Not that the robot had many accessories or even a name; it was simply a *jiqiren,* or machine-person. It was tall and ungainly and in the early days was just some hose and wires attached to a box, and for years the sound of Cao Cao's labors over it could be heard through the village, all that beating and hammering, and yet it never seemed to be done.

After a time, when they encountered Cao Cao, villagers would inquire after the *jiqiren* as they would a son who'd gotten himself into a difficult situation.

"How is the machine-person today?" they might ask, a touch of solicitousness in their manner.

"Not very obedient," Cao Cao would say, gritting his teeth, on the days that sparks flew and wires were twisted and retwisted until they frayed. On other days, though, he would beam proudly. "Very good! Just wait, soon Big Duck Village will have its very own machine-person to serve us."

At last, after six years, the robot was unveiled on a frigid December morning. The whole village turned up to watch as Cao Cao wheeled it out from his courtyard. The robot was built of a large silver-painted box with buttons across its torso, two legs made from fat piping, and new arms of soldered metal. His face was silver as well, with pink lips and black eyes and ears of pink cardboard. A white chef's hat sewn from an empty flour bag sat atop the robot's head, catching the pallid sunlight. One child exclaimed, "He's got a knife!" and so in fact he did: on his left arm, which was hinged, a piece of blunt metal rather like a letter opener had been affixed.

When Cao Cao placed a block of dough under it and activated the robot, the arm with the knife started to pump up and down, shaving the dough mechanically, yielding up a batch of even noodle strips. They were the kind of knife-cut noodles local to the area, easy to make, thick and chewy. At his side, his wife, Anning, stood shyly and caught the flying strips in a bowl.

A noodle-slicing robot! The crowd hadn't seen anything like it. Even Cao Cao and Anning's son had come back from town, an hour's drive away, to celebrate with them, even the party secretary had turned up. Some of the children came up and tried to touch the robot, and when they did, Anning shooed them briskly away, saying it wasn't a toy. Then she boiled the noodles and served them in bowls, a splash of vinegar and smashed garlic and chili oil thrown on top. She served the party secretary first, and Cao Cao tensed, awaiting his verdict.

"Chewy," he pronounced. "Delicious, Comrade Cao!"

It wasn't a term you heard much anymore, not like when Cao Cao had been in the army half a century ago. He often liked to think back to those days, back before the country had gotten rich. On the train ride out to join his company, at every stop, he and the men in camouflage had been greeted like conquerors: pretty girls cheering, offering them crackers and fruits. At one stop, he tasted an orange slice for the first time, a bright wedge of liquid barely held together by its skin, and as he released it between his teeth he nearly cried out in pleasure. Everyone was a comrade in those days, everyone a hero.

He'd hoped for a platoon, but because of the shortness of one leg he'd been assigned to the logistics division and chopped vegetables (mostly potatoes) for more than a year, fingers slick and aching. He'd been posted to a desert base three thousand miles away, where the sands stretched out interminably, and that was what he remembered most: gold sand, blue sky, planes taking off into that blue sky, and an endless parade of tubers to be chopped.

"Chairman Mao said to serve the people," Cao Cao told the assembled villagers earnestly. "With this machine-person, I hope to serve you good-tasting noodles."

That was a decade ago, and despite the party secretary's praise, Cao Cao's application for party membership was once again rejected that year, much to his disappointment. For a while one restaurant in town had rented the robot, with a big sign proclaiming ROBOT-SLICED NOODLES: CHEAP, MODERN, DELICIOUS. But the restaurant shuttered after the device lost its novelty, and the machine-person was sent back home to Cao Cao. It stood in their small kitchen, a hulking presence that mostly gathered dust, though occasionally women would run over if they were having a large family gathering. "Could we borrow your robot?" they'd ask, just as if they were asking to borrow a cleaver or a pan.

The airplane came to Cao Cao in a dream one night. In his dream he was flying in a silver contraption, not unlike the planes he'd seen take off during his army days. He was alone, and his knees felt weightless and a warm breath of wind hung all about his body.

He could move it at will, in diagonals, in graceful arcs, and he flew over the village, inspecting the rows of corn, the hills in the distance, and then, when night came, he bundled up a cloud in his arms like an infant and sang it softly to sleep.

The next morning, he started work on the airplane promptly, as though he'd been given a precise set of instructions. For months, Cao Cao's courtyard was again filled with the sound of hammering and sparks and motorized whirring. It would be a scaled-down plane, of course, just big enough to seat two people. But it would be a thing of beauty. He and Anning could ride it. As he grew older he found he grew more sentimental, and spoke more extravagantly of his love for her. "Such beautiful eyes," he'd say, staring at her over breakfast.

She'd snort. "Where was this nonsense when we first got married?" That had been a lifetime ago, another era. For their wedding, he'd given her parents a dowry of six chickens and three bags of Shanghai milled rice. The village had been poor then, subsisting on potatoes; rice of any kind—especially white—had been a luxury. Anning's strongest memory from the time was of standing outside the village toilet, waiting for a man with a shovel and pail to empty it. Every morning, she remembered, people waited for their allotment to spread in the fields, a dirty chore the children hated. In the summer, the stench rose like a thick cloud. In the winter, you could hear the sound of the shovel chipping away at the frozen mound.

"You are the love of my life and always have been," he'd say.

"We aren't teenagers," she'd reply, hiding her pleasure. "Go work on your airplane."

The neighbors found excuses to drop in so they could sneak looks at the contraption, which rose from the scraps Cao Cao had collected through the years like a metal phoenix, including parts of the old *jiqiren,* which the farmer had disassembled to make his plane. The reports circulated: It had wings built of hinged iron, or maybe steel. It had a rounded nose like the tip of an egg!

In the town nearest them, he bewildered shopkeepers with his requests and came back with new motors, cables, and sheet metal, even a red vinyl cushion for the pilot's seat. In time he had drained nearly all of his and Anning's savings, spending thousands of yuan. Anning fretted, and Cao Cao soothed her. When the airplane was ready, he said, they'd sell it at a profit. "There are rich men in town who might like to buy such a thing. With their own airplane, they can go anywhere. So convenient."

She said, "How do you know what rich men will like?"

Still, Cao Cao wasn't deterred. The party wanted members of standing, members of reputation, and surely once his plane was built, Secretary Jiang could not say no. If Cao Cao was a party member, everyone in the village would look at him differently. He would no longer be Cao Cao, a foolish old man whose son never returned to help with the harvest and whose cornfields always looked more ragged than the rest. He would be Cao Cao, a man who'd contributed to his village, to the nation's great revival, worthy of respect.

April came, and with it a week in which every villager scrabbled up into the mountains to gather apricots. It was an unspoken contest every year among all the residents, who kept a careful eye on the fruit's ripening. No one owned the land, and anyone could do the picking, but if anyone was watching, custom dictated you couldn't take more than your fair share. Early morning, then, was the best time; if you got there ahead of everyone else, the trees were still laden and you could pick more than your fill.

The apricot trees blossomed just before the summer, which was when the town party committee accepted party member recommendations from the countryside. For years, Cao Cao had woken early and climbed the hills to inspect the radiant white trees and their offerings. When the apricots were full and evidently ready for plucking, he would pick a whole bagful to present to the party secretary, keeping only a sticky handful in reserve for himself and Anning. Over the years, the simple transaction had gathered a tremendous significance in their eyes, though each tried to pretend it wasn't so.

"I probably won't be accepted this time," he'd tell her, as they sifted through the damp-skinned pile, picking out the roundest, the smoothest, leaving the dirt-scabbed ones behind.

"It's just to be polite," she agreed.

There were some in the village who didn't like the muskrat-faced man much; he never cleaned out his part of the sewer, leaving it to neighbors to take a stick and occasionally poke around to make sure the street didn't get backed up with his smelly refuse. It was whispered, too, that there were corn fertilizer subsidies the village was owed that had gotten stalled in the party secretary's pocket, though Cao Cao was among those who refused to listen. The party was responsible for the country's progress and prosperity — anyone could see that.

That year, in the week when the apricots began to beckon,

Cao Cao had woken up stiff and aching in his legs; every season, it seemed, the pain grew worse. On the third day, he lay in the cold room for a while, Anning's slow breathing beside him, before he forced himself upright in the direction of the hills. It wasn't yet dawn. As he climbed, his legs trembled, and he stopped in the blue dark and leaned against a boulder, heart hammering, uncertain. At last he pushed himself upward toward the white trees, but on arrival he saw others had been there before him: the branches were largely stripped.

Later in the day, he knocked tiredly on the party secretary's door. The house was the only one in the village that was tiled, mostly in white, though the entrance tiles were painted in red and green and turquoise flowers and dragons. When the party secretary opened the door, Cao Cao noticed that he was wearing a new, fine leather jacket, its grain soft and delicate as a woman's skin. Cao Cao ached to touch it.

Secretary Jiang asked about Anning and about his son, and then Cao Cao pulled out his half-filled bag. "It's not much," he said.

"Oh, no, I couldn't," the muskrat-faced man said. But Cao Cao noticed that his hand was already outstretched to take them. "And how's the plane coming along?" he asked.

Cao Cao beamed delightedly, encouraged. "It will be ready soon," he promised. "You will be the first to see it fly."

In the winter Cao Cao worked in a bulky coat and furry hat with earflaps, so that his face was scarcely visible. In the summer he worked in a white tank top and shorts that revealed wrinkled, skinny thighs. One morning he accidentally sprayed battery acid across his cheeks and neck, requiring a brief hospitalization in town. Their son, married now with a child, came to visit him, bringing with him apples and mimeographed sections of a book on airplane engineering. But he didn't stay long, and he didn't help peel the apples for his father, either.

"We should have had a daughter," Anning mourned as she left apple shavings on the ground. "A daughter you can depend on in your old age." For years, the village had been emptied of its young people; no one wanted to farm anymore. When they came back on weekends from town it was with tinny ringtones and asymmetrical bangs and white shoelaces, and they never stayed long.

After they got home from the hospital, the sky sulked for days, spitting rain, and when it came down harder, in great curtains, it made the roof leak. One night the wind blew loudly; it was as though a pack of ghosts was baying to get in. But then the sky cleared brilliantly, and Cao Cao worked for two months under a scrim of crystalline blue.

Sometimes he sang softly to himself. Years ago, the party secretary's father had died, and the whole village had been invited to his funeral. For a day the village's main street was lined with half a dozen sleek black cars draped in paper flowers and crowded with mourners who had come from five scattered villages over the mountain. There were cigarette packs handed around, and a giant framed portrait of the dead man that was carried by the party secretary and his family in a show of immense filial piety.

After the funeral and dinner and several speeches, a woman climbed onstage, and the audience quieted. A free meal would of course guarantee the attendance of everyone in the village, but getting mourners to honor the dead from farther away meant nighttime entertainment.

It was hot out, but the woman was wearing a high-necked red sweater, along with a red skirt trimmed with feathers and sparkles that caught the low light, and platform shoes. Someone turned on the stereo, and a fast-paced tune with a steady, recurrent beat blared, a love song. She began to dance, knees flashing forward and backward, as though she were a cantering pony. *"Can you can you can you can you see me, flying now straight into your heart."* Then, as the beat changed and grew slower, her moves grew languorous, catlike. She pouted. She shimmied one shoulder and rocked her body back and forth, using her pelvis as an anchor. Then she took off her sweater, tossing it to the crowd as though she couldn't be bothered with it. Beneath it was another red shirt, sparkling and sleeveless this time. In another minute, she'd stepped out of her skirt, too, which lay on the ground huddled in a feathery red pool like a forlorn tropical bird.

The crowd whooped and applauded. She arched her back, arms beating the air, and flipped her hair back and forth like she was trying to fan the crowd with her thick black tresses. Then she worked the red shirt above her shoulders and over her head, and that, too, went flying in the dark. She was down to just a red bra and her underwear now, gray with some sort of cartoon character on it.

She danced to one more song, a high-pitched Communist tune, and her steps grew more martial in their pacing. She turned to the left and stared into the sights of an imaginary rifle, and then repeated the same move to the right. "Platoon Leader Jiang, I salute you!" she shouted, and the crowd roared the same words back at her. She goose-stepped for a while in a circle, long enough for some of the men to notice that her calves and butt were skinny and that her eyes looked professionally bored.

Cao Cao had only ever heard the song that once, but he hummed it sometimes when he was happy, and he hummed it again now, working over his airplane: *"Can you can you can you can you see me, flying now straight into your heart."* He pictured the villagers' admiring stares and commentary as he unveiled his aircraft. He pictured it soaring up into the sky, just like the planes he'd seen take flight from the army base so long ago, then carefully adjusted the image to visualize the ground falling away, since he'd be the one flying it. It would place Big Duck Village on the map. It would be the pride of the village.

After months of work, at last the airplane stood in their courtyard, neat and trim, wings outstretched, like some strange insect that had alighted and hadn't yet decided whether to stick around. It had silver flaps and a metal body painted white with a jaunty red nose. He and Anning stood exhaling over their cups of tea, sending steam up into the air. It was done.

Word spread quickly. By the afternoon their courtyard was crowded with a dozen onlookers and an air of genial excitement. Cao Cao let them climb into the cockpit, one by one, to admire the joystick he'd installed and the controls, and the compass he'd soldered neatly to the dashboard.

Late in the afternoon, the party secretary came, too. He'd recently returned from a lavish party retreat at a mountain resort an hour's flight away, and offered tips to Cao Cao about his journey, in the tone of a seasoned hand. "When the plane takes off, you should expect some clogged feeling in your ears, and they might pop. That's normal — don't be alarmed," he said, patting the plane as though he'd built it himself. "And make sure you keep your seat belt fastened at all times, of course."

The girls from next door were there, too, grown up now, fourteen; they attended school in town. They still had their old habit, though, of speaking in tandem. "Can we see you fly?" they asked.

Cao Cao thought about it. His son wasn't there, or his grandchild, and they ought to be. And he still needed to install a seat belt. "Next weekend," he said. "Tell everyone!"

The next weekend was overcast, the sky a pearly gray. It required three younger men, their faces serious with their efforts, to get the airplane out from the courtyard, tipped on a diagonal through the double doors.

From there, they pushed the airplane out to the main road on the edge of the village. The crowd jostled around it excitedly. Cao Cao's phone rang continuously. First it was his daughter-in-law, saying that a photographer and reporter had arrived from town and that she'd sent them on to the test site. Then it was Anning, saying she was on her way as well and did he want his green hat — it would likely be cold up there. She was already bringing a scarf. She'd bring a thermos as well.

When she arrived at the juncture in the road she could scarcely see the plane, it was surrounded by so many villagers. Even youth who usually absented themselves in town for work or play had come back, Cao Cao was a figure of such fame in the village; many had been just children when he'd invented his noodle-slicing robot.

The cockpit was a little narrower than he'd intended, and it meant that when he and Anning climbed inside, they were pressed against each other uncomfortably. They'd both thickened in their old age. Still, once they were seated, a cheer went up from the crowd. The knitted scarf around Anning's neck was red and matched the plane's nose. Her eyes looked a little afraid and dazzled, by the attention as much as anything. The pink thermos containing chrysanthemum tea was wedged between her feet.

His son was shouting at the crowd, telling them to clear the way. His grandson was in his daughter-in-law's arms, blinking skyward, not seeing the scene. The crowd was cheering.

"Be careful!" his son shouted. "Do not fly too high!" They'd discussed it: a simple liftoff, and then come directly down. They weren't sure how quickly the fuel would burn.

With ceremony, Cao Cao scrupulously buckled the seat belt over his and his wife's laps. He grinned at the party secretary, who stood at the edge of the crowd, feeling a flush of pride at his presence. Then he pushed the throttle and the plane shot forward; it gathered speed, and then it was aloft—he could nearly feel it—but no, the ground was still bumping against them, they had not left the earth, and after another long minute they were approaching the end of the road, which dead-ended in a red-brick home that had NO DUMPING spray-painted on its side, and to avoid a crash, he abruptly slammed on the brakes. The party secretary's house, the largest in the village, was just to his right.

The crowd descended upon them, asking what had gone wrong. The photographer was snapping pictures.

A pit had begun to form in his stomach, but he ignored it. Out of the corner of his eye, he saw the party secretary frown. "Not to worry," he said. "I think it was something with the wings. Turn it around. We'll do it again."

They got laboriously out of the plane, Anning shaking out the cramps in her legs, and once again wheeled the plane around. Next to them, a dog was lifting its leg against the pavement. Their daughter-in-law was walking the baby back and forth in her arms, pointing at the sky for his amusement.

The plane turned around, he and Anning clambered back in. This time, he could not look at her. "You okay?" he asked.

"I left my thermos on the ground," she said in a small voice. When he turned his head, he could see it, a pink plastic cylinder sitting on the pavement with crumpled chrysanthemum blossoms floating inside.

"That's okay," he said reassuringly. "We'll get it later." He gritted his teeth, adjusted the wings, and hit the throttle again. The plane shot forward and gained speed. It also made a groaning noise, which didn't die down as it trundled forward and, once again, stayed stubbornly attached to the ground. They toodled on past the little shop that sold drinks and shampoo, past the public restrooms and rows of fields where yellowed, dried-out husks of corn stood in tall, stiff rows. When Cao Cao jerked it to a stop at the other edge of the village, the two of them sat frozen, with traces of scarlet creeping about Anning's cheeks, either from cold or shame, he couldn't tell.

"Maybe it's too heavy," Cao Cao said at last.

"Shall I get out?"

"I think that'd be best." The crowd was catching up behind

them. Anning climbed uncertainly out, and the boys once again turned the plane. "It was too heavy!" they shouted to the rest of the group. "Stand back!"

The crowd was a blur to Cao Cao, but if he tried to bring them into focus he could see children, the grave face of the party secretary, his friend Old Li, looking concerned. With increasing desperation, Cao Cao pressed the controls, and again the little aircraft trundled forward, rasping against the pavement. But the plane ran the length of the village — fields, restrooms, shop — and once more refused to go airborne.

Behind him, he could hear the footsteps of the crowd pounding to catch up. "What's the problem?" he heard someone shout. "It won't fly!" someone else said.

The reporter, a young woman with green spectacles, ran up to him with a pen. "Old Cao," she said, "did you expect this to happen? Has the plane ever taken off successfully before? How much did you spend to make this plane?"

He sat and stared straight ahead into the camera lens as her photographer arrived and stood in the plane's path, clicking away; it was easier than looking at the crowd. A great wasteland of sorrow was opening up in him, unfolding dozens of tiny shacks, terrible squatters setting up residence, banging their miniature liquor bottles against his chest, a hundred feet trampling his organs. It was the same feeling he'd had as a teen when his father had died, a suicide during a year of bad harvest, and only a dirt mound to mark his grave. He'd failed. He'd failed. He'd have to try again.

Cao Cao climbed out of the cockpit, dismay and unhappiness clinging to him like dirty rain. "Friends," he said, "it seems there may be some problem I didn't anticipate. I am sorry for those I have inconvenienced today," he said. "I know many of you have come from far away."

There was a long silence. Old Li looked at him worriedly and scanned the crowd. The party secretary was checking his watch. "What is everyone so long-faced about?" Old Li said, hurriedly. "It may not be a bird, but it is certainly a beast!"

"Speak clearly, Old Li!" someone else shouted.

"What are you talking about?"

"It's a car!" he gasped. "Cao Cao has invented a car!"

The crowd turned to look at the little contraption with its wings outstretched, fat-bodied and content, more bee than butterfly. It wasn't a very good airplane. But it might be a pretty good car.

"Neat," said one of the youth who had come home to see the show. "Can I ride it?"

It was a girl with purple-streaked hair who worked at an internet café in town. She was wearing white heels and a shiny silver coat. Cao Cao could remember her as a plump girl who liked to play with the village dogs when she was small, who until age five seemed in fact confused about whether she was girl or canine, and used to bark when spoken to. "Sure," he said now, swallowing with gratitude. "Come on, I'll take you."

She climbed up and Cao Cao buckled her in. The duo shot off across the main street again, her purple streaks of hair flying in the wind like flames. "This is great," she said as they skimmed along the road, past the shop, the restrooms, and the fields of corn. "Actually, it's better than flying," she said. "I've been on a plane before."

"Oh, really?"

"It's like you're sitting in a room the whole time," she said. "You don't really feel it. It isn't like you'd expect."

"The party secretary said it was amazing," he said.

"The party secretary," she said, "is an idiot."

When they coasted to a stop, she alighted daintily in her white heels. "Thank you, Cao Cao!" she said, and walked off, leaving him staring.

Later that night, he and Anning lay in bed under their duvet, which had started life as a white blanket trimmed with pink flowers but had since gone gray with dirt and age. The moonlight spilled in from the window across the floor. Beside him, Anning's snores vibrated the room. Cao Cao turned on his side and tried to make out her outline. In the darkness it was easier to pretend that neither of them had aged, that it was just the two of them, twenty years old and childless; life had yet to leave its scars on their bodies, they lay as pure and fresh as infants.

He thought about what the girl with the purple hair had said to him about the party secretary, and the corners of his mouth moved. The next day, he thought, he would change the throttle. He would check the engine. He would make the thing fly, he thought. Next time, he wouldn't invite anyone to watch.

He closed his eyes, but sleep eluded him. Instead he lay on his back and carefully imagined himself walking through his storeroom, which held years of the village's trash. He could see the woven plastic sacks that had held the grain that sustained them once in a year of disastrous famine. He could see the broken bicycle wheels of two different newlywed couples, betrothal gifts discarded after they'd outworn their use. He could see the extra pipe lengths from when the village got its first cisterns and a bag of rags his neighbor had given him, old clothes torn into strips after his girls had grown up and grown out of them.

He saw them all, and in his head he rearranged them. There was a washing machine to be built out of bicycle wheels and pipes and the oil drum in one corner. There was a robot dog. There was a set of foam cushions he could turn into shoes that walked on water. There was a trash compactor he could build that would crush it all into tiny cubes that he would carefully stack, one by one, until they made a perilous tower that he could scale to the sky.

ON THE STREET
WHERE YOU LIVE

WHEN I SEE HIM, THE MAN WITH THE MEAL CART IS COMING AT ME WITH A TRAY, CREAMED SPIN-ACH, WATERY MASHED POTATOES, AND A SPLATCH OF MEAT LIKE A THICK PIECE OF RUBBER. I sit up obediently, straighten the front of my jumpsuit, and smile. *I am an observer of your country, I am a great admirer of your country,* I think, and surely he might, on this seventh day of days, take notice. "Hello," I say, and wave my hand.

I position myself in an attitude of readiness for conversation, but he simply slides the tray through the slot and moves on, pushing his cart.

He is not singing. No one is singing. It is fetid and damp and grim, and yesterday I saw a rat, an actual rat, scurry across the corridor. If this were a movie the rat would be white as snow and there would be a dozen of them and they'd turn into horses, all ready and pawing and whining in their eagerness to pull a pumpkin turned carriage. If this were a musical I would lead our row in a soft-shoe shimmy, a graceful bow at the waist, a flick of the wrist.

The only person in my line of sight is Bruce, though, who must be eighty pounds heavier than me and spends his time mostly staring at the walls in the cell opposite. Bruce is here for an ugly, brutal crime, and has no interest in dancing.

But then, I am getting distracted, I am losing track of the thread. I have always liked that expression, the image that it conjures. I picture myself crawling about the mess hall (except there is no mess hall in this wing) seeking out its elusive, tapered end, making soft apologies, checking behind sneakers: "Sorry, sorry, excuse me, thank you, sorry." *That's how long I've been in your country,* I think *—apologies and gratitude spring forth from me at any opportunity.*

Thank you, sir, for the spinach and potato gruel and for this rubber.

I had hoped, of course, to be of assistance to the police. I have made it my practice to study the law in any country I call a place of abode. I am an extremely educated man. I have two degrees, one of which is useless—I am certainly no accountant—and another, in design, which has served me in great stead. By the time I

was twenty-nine, I had lived in five different countries: two as I was
shuttled between different boarding schools in Europe, three more
at the Hongxi conglomerate, a name that by now is surely familiar to you; perhaps it supplies your cable connection, or owns the
local shopping mall. When I first joined, the company motto, *We
Bring You the World,* seemed a comic overstatement; now as I sit here
writing, it seems precise.

I will tell you how I really met Perry. It was the end of the day,
a long day, and when I came home he was on my front stoop waiting for me. No, not for me, exactly, but for Lisette. My Lisette. They
had dated before and he'd come back to her old apartment, heart
in his throat, hoping foolishly to see her. I told him he should have
checked the address and slammed the door in his face. This country can be dangerous. He could have been armed. A man is very
dangerous if he is armed and thinks you are keeping his beloved
inside.

"Blue eyes," he'd said, shouting through the door. "Five-seven.
She had glasses and dirty-blond hair."

How disrespectful to speak of her that way, I thought. *So much shouting.
And* dirty-blond, *what a choice of words! He surely wouldn't speak of his
mother that way,* I thought. I turned the blinds and snapped them
shut. *Come back later,* I thought imperiously. *Come back never.*

It is true the apartment was not very nice. In Barcelona, I lived
in an apartment that was on the eighteenth floor and had a black-
and-white-tiled lobby and dormer windows bathed in sheer white
fabric. There was a bakery below that served croissants warm and
soft and many-layered as you pulled them apart, like the under-
belly of a sea creature gently exhaling. There was a man and woman

above me who periodically had exuberant, ceiling-thumping relations that made me blush. In Beijing, our apartment looked out over the wide gray mélange of the city from the twenty-seventh floor of a concrete skyscraper called Harmony Estates, with fake flowers in the foyer and white columns somewhat unexpectedly surging up from our front entrance.

Lisette's street was three miles from Atlantic City's casinos and resorts, low-slung and crossed with saltwater breezes that left the hair and face sticky, all porches and driveways and scraggly lawns. Nothing special, but farther out, the city spruced itself up and suited me fine. Most weekends I took in a show: the high kicks, the high-singing warblers, all the jubilant notes. Strut, pose, *rat-a-tat-tat!* In America, neighborhoods like Lisette's are the backstage; downtown is where the performance really happens. I liked knowing the backstage, too.

Perry came back the next afternoon. He was sitting on my front steps and eating a sandwich wrapped in white butcher paper when I returned from work.

"Sorry," he said, though he didn't sound sorry at all, just demanding. "I really have to find this girl. How long have you been living here?"

I'd stopped a few paces away, looking around us. It was five o'clock, late-afternoon sunlight. There was the tinkling sound of an ice cream vendor down the block. Ms. Castle, who lives in the white house opposite, was eyeing us as she went to her car.

"Not long," I said defensively.

"Her name is Lisette," he said, as though I'd been asking after her. "She used to live here."

"So you said." It had been a hot day at the park inspecting a river-rapids ride, our newest attraction, and I was tired.

"I love her," he said.

"If you love her, shouldn't you have her telephone number?"

"Not necessarily," he said, and offered me a part of his sandwich. "Anyway, she isn't picking up."

"That's your problem," I said, and went past him, shutting the door. I always liked that phrase, the neat apportioning of its logic.

Perry kept popping up after that in the afternoons, sitting on my porch as though he genuinely had no idea of where else to go. Sometimes he rang my doorbell. Usually he was eating some kind of takeout: often it was a pastrami sandwich, occasionally orange chicken with rice. Did the man never eat indoors? Or was he just eating all the time? He didn't look it. He had red hair and spidery freckles and was tall and very, very skinny. He had terribly, sharply flared nostrils, like a woman's short skirt as it billows during a merengue.

He was very insistent. Spoiled simpleton!

I bet Perry would not have dared go on my ride. He would have gone instead for an old-fashioned roller-coaster, or hung around the concession stand, his beloved, lost Lisette beside him, tenderly ministering popcorn. He did not look like a man who could stomach life's indignities, whether it was a closed door or an uncomfortable, vertigo-inducing passage through a birth canal.

I'm talking, of course, about the Tunnel of Love. At the time I joined, Hongxi had just begun buying up film studios and shopping malls across the globe. Its owner, Kang Jun, was a glib, unattractive man who looked like a stretched-out toad with a surprisingly firm handshake. He had been in the military. He had known my father there, and that's how I got this job. I think he'd assumed I was going to be a vanity hire, like so many of the others who went abroad. I flatter myself, except it is no flattery, that I surprised him.

The Tunnel of Love was for a while the showcase in Hongxi's newly opened theme park in the outskirts of Beijing. Now, of course, you see the ride copied elsewhere, but at the time you must remember it had not been done before. Riders were shrouded in plastic and blindfolded. They lay on gurneys and were strapped in. Then they were taken through a writhing, heated machine that would tighten around them in a fashion progressively more painful and uncomfortable, as they fought to reach the other side. On the way, shuddering and writhing through such contractions, they were submerged in a hot, viscous liquid that rippled all around them. The whole experience took six minutes. "Relive life's original trauma!" was how we advertised it. "In birth, we find ourselves alive." In English, when we opened the theme park overseas, the placard that greeted riders on the other side simply read WELCOME TO THE WORLD. In Madrid, it was BIENVENIDOS AL MUNDO!

Some thought it was crude, of course, or tasteless. But you'd be surprised, the way some people emerged from it, weeping, others stepping out, blinking with wonder, as though they'd found a new courage to go on with life. Isn't it the most remarkable thing, to remember where we came from? Isn't that something we all secretly crave?

One morning, before work, Perry found me at the coffee shop. He lurched in and immediately sat down at my table.

"I am really sorry to keep bothering you," he said. His face looked red and flushed, his cheek creased from his pillow that morning. *What an unattractive man,* I thought. "I just need to find her, and I have no idea where else to go. She didn't leave a forwarding address? Do you ever get any of her mail?"

I looked at him, considered him. He was wearing a green sweater. He didn't look like a madman. He looked like a man in distress. He also didn't seem inclined to leave me alone.

"How did you know her, anyway?" I asked. For a moment I closed my eyes and pictured her. She had very ordinary hands, Lisette, I remembered that: a little plump, a little fat, like sugar cookies that hadn't been properly rolled out, and hair so fine it felt like water. She had a body that wasn't extraordinary, a little squat. Big blue eyes, though, as blue as any starlet's.

"I told you, we dated," he said. "Before I went to Abu Dhabi." He was jiggling his knees now, looking anxious and hectored. He took a piece of biscotti off my plate without asking and nibbled it before realizing what he was doing and put it down, abruptly.

"And?"

"And nothing," he said grumpily, as though I'd overstepped my bounds. "We got into an argument — we stopped talking. But I'm back now, and I thought I might be able to make it up to her."

"When did you last see her?"

"Four years ago," he said. "I guess it's longer ago than it seems." He paused and eyed my biscotti again. "Are you going to eat that?" I slid the plate over to him wordlessly.

"Lisette doesn't live there anymore," I said.

"I got that," he said. "I just wanted to know, do you have any of her mail or anything? Something that might have a return address, someone else who might know how to find her."

Finally I acquiesced. "Okay," I said. "Come by tomorrow evening. I'll take a look."

My mother once told me that everything is an opportunity for self-improvement, and in prison I am wise to that fact, I am an eager pupil. In the mornings I fold my blanket into a fat, even rectangle and scrub my sink until it's utterly blameless. I do push-ups and walk around my cell chanting, "What ho, what ho!" but softly, so the other inmates won't object. The true measure of a man is how he responds to adversity, I tell myself. I am fit, polite, and neat. I am a good guest, good company.

Today a guard brought in a new prisoner, his arms shackled —best not to wonder about his crimes. He was a big man, with crude, tattooed dashes inked across his arms and thick black lines running jagged across his neck, as though his body were sewn together. It was so ugly, I couldn't bear to look. It's so ugly here.

In the afternoons I sit quietly and think of Lisette. I know the science: if you do not regularly relive your memories, they will disappear, and so I sit and pore over them by the hour; it passes the time. Every few minutes, I change my posture, to stop my limbs from falling asleep.

We met during my second year in the city. She was a not-very-competent receptionist in a doctor's office and was studying Mandarin, which she was not very good at, either, but she'd turned up at a dinner a coworker was hosting and amused us all with her attempts to chatter away in the language, even as the rest of us were speaking English and had been schooled abroad, knew all the cultural reference points. I guess I stared at her most of that evening. It wasn't that I thought she was particularly good-looking—she wasn't, especially. But I thought—I don't know how else to express it—that she looked kind. She laughed a lot, and easily. It wasn't until we actually became friends that I realized she was often very sad. America is like that, I must say, free and easy until you know better.

In the months after that, Lisette and I spent long afternoons at her apartment. Sometimes we'd watch old films or I'd give her language lessons, sometimes I just watched her out of the corner of my eye as we read on separate couches, like a prematurely old married couple. The place was an odd jumble. One room held a substantial collection of stuffed animals that tumbled off the shelves: white bears with velvet skirts, a floppy-limbed frog, a menagerie of cotton batting and differently colored furs. In a half-whisper, as though anxious not to wake them up, she'd recite their names and brief biographies: this one a birthday gift from her stepfather, that one won while playing arcade games on a family vacation.

"Don't laugh at me," she said. I wouldn't have dreamed of it.

Before I met Lisette, America wasn't what I'd imagined; it's only natural, I expect. Everyone was friendly, but bafflingly so, as though each person had a series of invisible hedges around them that I didn't know how to penetrate. Lisette was different, you see. She needed me, wanted me.

Between periods of great buoyancy, she complained of phantom illnesses. A few months after we met, a man she'd been seeing had stopped calling, and as a consequence she had several weeks of unexplained pain in her side. It meant she called in sick, couldn't leave her couch. It meant that I had every excuse and opportunity to come minister to her, which I did, enthusiastically. Twice I accompanied her to the emergency room when her symptoms worsened. Even then I already suspected there was nothing very wrong with her, but her eyes were squeezed shut in pain and she was gripping my hand and I could have sat there for hours more, the way she clung to me, hair slightly matted on her forehead like a child with a fever.

I missed work and didn't mind. After the Tunnel of Love's initial success, Hongxi wanted me to design more rides; they'd sent me to Europe, to Australia. I'd had other ideas, lots of them. But all they wanted were flying ladybugs, Tilt-A-Whirls, and the like. I had no interest! These days an amusement park shouldn't just fling people about on mechanical arms, I told them. There were new VR technologies that would allow us to conjure up any environment: a glamorous cocktail party, bullets whizzing on a battlefield, even (yes!) a bridal chamber. These days, people wanted more: to feel connected, to taste life deeply!

Instead, after six years they moved me to a back office here in Atlantic City and gave me a new title, quality inspector, and I spent days in the field with a clipboard making careful ticks.

Lisette had spark. I wanted to be around her all the time. I bought gifts that I pressed her to accept. I lent her money I knew she wouldn't return. Late one night, when I couldn't sleep, I parked outside her apartment and sat there for hours, show tunes on the stereo: *"Are there lilac trees in the heart of town? No, it's just on the street where you live."*

One of my most treasured memories of Lisette was the day we

were sitting on her couch, blue-and-red-and-white-flowered up-holstery. I had a notepad on my knee, a few inches from hers, and was tracing out a set of characters.

"*Maotouying,*" I read aloud.

I watched Lisette's lips, dry and chapped, form the syllables. The sunlight was bright and unkind, and the skin under her eyes looked like wrinkled crepe, but I didn't mind. She was Eliza before her transformation, and I liked her better that way. It took a certain kind of man, I flattered myself, to see her potential.

"It means 'cat-headed eagle,'" I told her. She cocked her head slightly and thought before shaking her head, stumped.

"An owl," I said.

She laughed. "No way," she said, and hit me lightly on the side of my arm; it was the kind of gesture of hers that drove me crazy, at once sisterly and flirtatious. "That's actually really good."

"Okay, now *changjinglu.*"

"*Changjinglu.*"

"Long-necked deer."

"A giraffe?"

"You got it," I said. We both laughed, and I tapped my pen and tried to think of more.

The window was to our backs, white sill gritty with dust from outside. She was so close that if I'd leaned over just a little, our shoulders would have touched. Then, without warning, she reached out and gently traced the blurred outline of my right ear, crumpled and flattened. It was a congenital defect, with me since birth. As a child, at my mother's suggestion, I'd tried growing out my hair to cover it; the effect was not good.

"Neat," she said casually. She said it felt like a melted candle. "So soft," she said, as I held my breath and tried not to breathe on her. I'd had garlic at lunch that day but hadn't had a chance to brush my teeth yet, and for that suspended moment I felt simultaneously absurd, sordid, and blessed. *Why didn't I order the soup? Or the salad?*

That night, most thrillingly of all, after we'd watched two movies and I'd gotten up to leave, she turned to me. "You don't have to go," she said, and it was like a great gift had been handed to me, along with the blanket she tossed carelessly my way as she went to her room. Later, I lay in the dark on her couch, listening to the sound of the water as she took a shower. When she opened the door, a yellow rectangle of light spilled out and there she was, wrapped in a towel, pausing in the frame as though she could sense my excitement. My heart stopped. Little tease!

I inhaled in anticipation and began to sit up, but she was already disappearing into her room and sealing the light behind her.

After that, I slept fitfully. At last around 3 a.m., unable to contain myself, I got up and went to her bedroom door, listening for any sound, imagining her prone within. When I agitated the handle, though, it refused to move.

After I returned from the coffee shop, I deliberated a long time over what piece of mail to give Perry. There were bags and bags of it: the glossy fashion magazines that had continued to arrive for six months until finally her subscriptions must have been canceled, the credit card bills made out to her name, and many more of that genre. There was a wedding invitation from a friend in Minnesota

—I knew it was a wedding invitation because I'd opened it—but the fact that it had been opened was obvious; the envelope was all ripped. The next morning, I stopped in a stationery store and bought another square white envelope that mostly matched, copied the addresses in careful script, and resealed it.

When I handed it to Perry that night as he stood on my porch, he looked at it and caressed its edges. "Finally," he breathed. He looked like he wanted to rub it against his face. "Is that all?"

"You can't open it," I told him, a little primly, not answering him. "That's a federal offense, opening someone else's mail."

He shrugged and slid his finger under the flap. "Well, don't tell anyone."

He opened the envelope and I watched his face as he removed the thick ivory card inside. The wedding invitation said *Portia Vaughn and David Cohen request the pleasure of your company* and had letters wrapped in fingers of ivy.

"You didn't need to open it," I told him. I was angry that he hadn't listened to me, such an unmannered person. "I thought all you wanted was the return address."

He turned over the invitation and the envelope, examining them. "Hey," he said. "It's not stamped."

My chest thudded a little—how could I have forgotten that? —but I kept calm. "Weird," I said. "Maybe they hand-delivered it."

"The return address is all the way in Minnesota," he said. I shrugged and tried to contain the urge to rip the card out of his hands. I started to close the door, but he stuck his foot in it. "Wait," he said. "I'm not feeling very well. Can I have a glass of water?"

I stared at his foot; I didn't like his foot there. But it was such a reasonable request. I went inside and got him a glass and sat opposite him at the kitchen table as he drank it, the two of us very silent. I could see him looking around the room. I shouldn't have poured him such a tall glass, I thought. He seemed determined to finish every drop, as though it would be an affront to waste any of it.

At this point in the script, a man might slam his fist on the table, race through the rooms, and demand answers. He did not. He just sat there, drinking and looking around.

"Are you sure you didn't know her?" he said, looking at me oddly. "I swear, some of this furniture looks exactly the same." He was staring at one plant in the corner, green leaves touched with brown, which stood in an orange pot. "Like, that plant. I guess maybe it was the landlord's?"

"I told you, I haven't lived here that long," I said stiffly. And somehow the act of speaking broke the spell, and I was able to get up, indicating to him that he, too, should leave.

He was smiling now. "Okay, okay, I'll go. Thanks for this," he said, patting the envelope.

"No problem," I muttered, and shut the door behind him.

Six months after I'd met Lisette, there came a Saturday morning when I did not expect to see her. But then there was a buzz at my apartment and her voice sudden and warm on the intercom, saying she was downstairs. I let her up and began rushing around the room, kicking dirty laundry under the bed, madly stacking dishes in the sink.

When I opened the door, she was standing there, staring at me with a strange intensity in her blue eyes. "I'm going away," she said, smiling. "I've decided."

I felt the excitement that had fizzed up inside me subside. "Already? You just got here."

"Not *now*," she said. She walked in and threw herself on the couch. "In a couple weeks. I'm leaving town."

My stomach dropped, as if all the muscles and sinews that had been keeping it suspended abruptly forgot their roles.

"What?"

"I'm going to start over," she said. "Like the pioneers. I'm going to move away."

I stared at her stupidly, still standing. "Where?" I only seemed capable of speaking in one-word questions.

She shrugged. "I don't know yet. But I'm going away, I'm going to start a new life."

"Why?"

"I'm tired of my life here," she said. She kicked off her shoes and began wiggling her toes. "I'm moving away. New life. New identity."

"What happened?" I said, half wondering if this was a game.

She frowned, and admitted that she'd been fired from her office the previous day. "But that's not why I'm leaving," she said. "I just want to start over. And I'm going to need your help," she said.

"Why me?"

"Because you're my friend," she said impatiently, "and I can trust you." She went to the kitchen and began rifling through the refrigerator.

Lisette was helpless in a lot of ways, but she was also canny, and she knew, I think, that I'd do most anything for her. In the weeks that followed, she was hyper, talking constantly about her plans. She'd wake up early and call me, buzzing with one idea or another. One day she purchased maps, lots of maps. Another day she threw out all of her books and lamps, left them outside on the sidewalk.

"Why are you doing this?" I kept asking her, to which she'd shrug.

"I've been so bored," she said. "I've been stuck."

In the last week before she left, I took off work and helped her clear out her apartment, arranging her things into tidy piles. The stuffed animals went to Goodwill, along with assorted furnishings and six bags of clothes. "I still need to pay my landlord for the rest of this month," she hesitated, not looking at me.

"I can handle it," I told her. She'd been sitting opposite me on the floor, sorting through a stack of papers, and when I said that, she rose up on her knees and hugged me unsteadily. "Thank you," she breathed into my closed-up right ear. "I don't know what I'd do without you."

The day before Lisette left, I managed to persuade her to come see our amusement park. She hadn't wanted to, she was exhausted, she said, but after all I'd done, I'd insisted and she said yes. I wanted the day out, just the two of us, wanted her to see the place where I was host and the locals were guests, enjoying the rides that I'd made. At the park, we ate funnel cake and roasted peanuts. To my surprise, though, Lisette stubbornly refused to go into the Tunnel of Love. She shuddered, looking at it. "No thanks."

"It's my invention," I told her. "This is how I started my career, back in Beijing."

"You never told me that."

"I'm sure I did," I said. "Never mind. Try it. You'll be wrapped in plastic—you won't get too wet."

"I'm okay," she said. "I don't like enclosed spaces."

"You'll like it, I swear," I told her. "It's about rebirth. What it's like to experience a moment in your life that most of us have forgotten. Come on—I'll do it with you." I tried pulling her by the arm.

She'd been sulky all day, exhibiting no interest in the details of the park that I'd pointed out, the Hongxi baseball cap that I'd bought her. "Quit pushing me around," she said suddenly.

She stalked away, hands in her coat pockets. I followed her at a distance, feeling panicky at first but also excited—like maybe this was the time to make a gesture of some kind: sweep her into my arms, maybe, stammer out a confession of how I felt! We could ride the Ferris wheel as the sun went down, the sky pulled over us like a blanket, we could share a doughnut, me brushing the powdered sugar from her cheek as we dangled in the air.

When I caught up with her, though, she had stopped to buy a corn dog and was eating at a picnic table that crawled with ants, and she didn't look happy to see me. We sat there silently until she finished, and when she suggested we go on a ride called the Sunflower Bunnies, a bunch of white bunny rabbits with seats indented in their bellies that rose dolefully up and down on brass poles, a ride designed for five-year-olds—it wasn't (mercifully) my work—I didn't argue with her and got on. We sat on two opposite bunny laps, not bothering to belt ourselves in, rising up and down miserably, not speaking.

"Sorry," she said, as we walked out of the ride. "I don't know why I get like that sometimes." She shifted uncomfortably. "Let's go home," she said. "I'm starting to feel a stomachache coming on."

I still don't understand why she wanted to leave. To be honest, up until she was getting into her old used car, white with a MY GRANDSON IS AN HONORS STUDENT AT STILES HALL sticker on its bumper, I thought she'd turn back: Just kidding, an aborted experiment, just another emergency-room visit, this one involving a tank of gas and several large duffel bags. I'd participated in the charade, pushing her to take extra bottles of water, an emergency blanket so that she could sleep in the car.

"Where are you going to go?" I kept asking, but up until she got into the driver's seat, she said she didn't know. She'd call me later, she said impatiently, she'd figure it out on the road.

That afternoon, I let myself into her apartment with her key and spent the rest of that day lying on her flowered couch, and for days after that I kept coming back. If I half closed my eyes or kept them turned a certain way, it was possible to imagine that Lisette was just in the next room, or perhaps in the bathroom, emptying her delicate bowels. Eventually I gave up my apartment across town and fixed it with her landlord that I could keep staying at her place. I liked it there. I'd even gone to the Goodwill to buy back some of Lisette's things: the orange ceramic mugs she used, kitchen towels, some of her stuffed animals.

Weeks went by. I didn't hear from Lisette, and when I called, she didn't pick up, either.

It took a long time for me to realize she wasn't ever going to call, and when that knowledge sank in, for a while it undid me; it was like I was new to the city all over again. I felt pinpricks of despair that felt harder and harder to brush away, sticky like a Hollywood rain, water mixed with milk so it shows on the screen.

I found new pursuits. In the months after she left, I fell into the habit of wandering the strip downtown, picking out women here and there, following them when they caught my eye, never to their front steps, never approaching them, nothing like that, but sometimes you see a girl by herself and simply wonder: Where is she going? What is her life? And sometimes it is a soothing thing, to fall into the rhythm of another person's step. There is no violation here of the law.

Only once was I spotted: a pale blonde with a pointed face who, after an hour, called over a casino security guard, who spoke briefly into his walkie-talkie before accosting me. Up close, the woman's mouth, small and dry, bore a trite expression of outrage. When the guard demanded my business, I told him I was lost and needed directions. He shook his head in disbelief. "You'd better get out of here," the guard said warningly, and gave the woman a look that struck me as unnecessarily protective.

As I walked away, the woman muttered, loud enough so that I could hear, "Freak."

I walked a few more steps, face hot, and when I was far enough away I turned and faced the pair again, the word surging out of my mouth: "Whore!"

At the trial, Ms. Castle, who keeps a close eye on the neighborhood, told the courtroom that Perry had spent days waiting for me outside my apartment, and that we appeared to be quarreling, and that I would shut the door in his face. On two separate occasions he had gone inside, she says, once late at night.

It is not a story I relish and so I will tell you quickly.

The next time I saw Perry was, of all places, at the opera. A colleague of mine had tickets from an investor. We sat through two hours of a woman with a big head and big hair screeching, and finally my colleague left to take a phone call and didn't return. I sat until the end and filed out with the crowd, Perry among them. I very nearly didn't recognize him. His red hair had been brushed flat. He was wearing a black coat with a white pinafore-style shirt and bow tie, far more dressed-up than anyone in the room. We sighted each other in the red-carpeted lobby, with its graceful marble urns and yellow lights winking above. I was wearing a simple business suit. It had been three months since I'd seen him, and we greeted each other like embarrassed, long-lost acquaintances.

He split off from the woman who was with him — perhaps his sister, I thought; she shared the same ruddy hair — and then he was outside with me on the pavement and we were walking.

The night was cool and velvety and inviting. Perry was at my side, and we were both silent. "Where are you headed?" I asked at some point, and he shrugged. "Nowhere in particular," he said. "I'll walk with you." And so he kept walking with me, past the hotels and bars, past the sleeping gas stations and shuttered shops with their graffitied grills, all the way back to my street and up my front steps, then across the threshold, and inside. On the way, he told me about what the desert looked like in the Middle East, and about the hot air like a hair dryer in your mouth, about how the cars there came with devices that beeped incessantly whenever you went over the speed limit, which for him was most days. I told him about growing up in Beijing, the dusty gray of the skies, the freezing winters, and how the rain left dirty scrawls on my father's fleet of expensive black cars, how I used to like taking a wet paper towel and cleaning them, the meditative feel of the gesture.

Inside, I flicked the lights on, and the couch, Lisette's bookshelves, my boots and papers all sprang into focus, like they'd been startled in the middle of some act.

"Are you hungry?" I asked uncertainly. He looked like a character from a movie, still wearing his tuxedo, ill suited to his surroundings. "I have toast. I could make you some eggs."

He nodded. "Sure, that'd be great."

I went into the kitchen and started taking out ingredients. He stayed in the living room, where, out of the corner of my eye, I could see him pacing around, inspecting things. I worried, irrationally, that he might wander into the bedroom and perhaps see Lisette's stuffed animals, the ones I'd rescued from Goodwill, lining my bookshelf.

"Hey," I called. "Come and talk with me."

He came in and folded himself, like a lanky piece of origami, against the doorframe. "Need any help?"

I gave him a grater and a knob of cheese and he silently started working it against the metal. I turned back to the stove, where the skillet was starting to smoke and the wedge of butter I'd cut had softened and was turning brown. I threw in six eggs and a cascade of salt, too much salt. "Sorry," I said. "I'm not a very good cook."

He appeared at my side and dropped in the cheese. The kitchen was getting warm. Perry stripped off his coat and opened the pantry door slightly and hung his coat over the top, as if it were something he'd done many times before. After the eggs had fluffed themselves up in the pan, I turned the omelet upside down and divided it in two before pulling out forks from the cutlery drawer. They were Lisette's and didn't match.

We ate in silence. I'd uncorked a bottle of red wine, and we were both drinking steadily. I asked him about the wedding invitation, about Portia and David, if he'd ever heard back. "They never replied," he said, a little sheepishly. "I guess they might think it was kind of weird, someone they'd never heard of looking for her like that."

He was working as a consultant now, he said, living with his sister. It was hard to readjust to life here. "Everyone works so hard," he said. "Everyone expects you to be on top of your game." It was lonely, he said. He'd been feeling lonely for two months before that day I'd first found him sprawled out on the porch, asking for Lisette.

"I guess it was a little pathetic," he said.

"Not at all."

"I guess you must feel lonely, too, coming all the way from China," he said.

I told him not so much, honestly, that I'd left home so young I felt lonely when I went back there, too.

I told him about the Tunnel of Love, and he brightened. "That's what I need, a new start," he said, and gave a laugh like the bark of a dog, a dog that was a little old, a little sick. I told him I'd take him there sometime. We were a little tipsy by then, I suppose. I told him that I'd been thinking about creating a cradle experience, an infant experience, for our parks. A crib that you could lie inside, with a giant mobile suspended above your head softly playing nursery tunes, and maybe a couple of giant faces that would peer down at you every so often and coo.

Perry looked at me strangely then, but nodded, trying to be agreeable. "Sure," he said. "I guess that sounds kind of nice."

Afterward we wiped the dishes together in the kitchen, Perry automatically reaching for the drawer where Lisette had kept the towels. They were the same red-and-white-striped ones she'd used before, but he must not have noticed, I thought; anyway, he didn't comment on it. It was late, and the wine had gone to my head, and maybe his as well. He pulled open the pantry door to pick his coat up, and as he did, he paused and said a hoarse, "Hey."

It was the mail. All the accumulated stacks of Lisette's mail, which I had kept tumbled in bags in the pantry and somehow that evening had forgotten about. I stopped breathing, suddenly panicked, suddenly afraid.

After she'd left, I guess Lisette must have changed her phone number, because whenever I called, it just rang and rang. Still, I was getting her credit card statements, and for a while I watched her travel across the country: a cheap motel here, a quarter-tank of gas there, a hot dog with fries, never staying anyplace very long. After a few months, I could see where Lisette had wound up, a small town of two thousand people—no, I won't tell you where—a town where she lived and worked and bought groceries, all carefully itemized, down even to the address of where she pumped her gas, every page a postcard. For months before Perry had turned up, I had nursed fantasies of going out there.

"It's not hers," I said stupidly, my brain thick and slow.

"Of course it is," he said. "Why didn't you tell me? Maybe there's something useful here." He knelt and began turning envelopes over.

"Stop it," I said. "It's mine." Perry was picking it up, great handfuls of mail, sifting through and cramming pieces of it into his coat pockets, ignoring me.

I shoved him, but he didn't move. "Stop it," I said, panic rising. I tried grabbing the mail from his hands, but he pushed me aside easily and stood up, panting slightly.

"What the hell is wrong with you?" he said.

I don't know what to tell you. My blood surged then, hot, and for a moment my vision got all funny like it was overlaid with a thin vellum, for a moment I couldn't see. "Come back here," I cried, but he had already left the kitchen and was pacing around the apartment, as though looking for someone.

He was in my room, Lisette's room, with its big bookshelf still lined with her stuffed animals, the orange throw pillow that had been hers as well. He was opening up the closets, looking under the bed. I stood outside the door helplessly, my heart pounding like it was trying to escape and screamed: "Trespass! Trespass!"

"Jesus," I heard him say, from inside.

When he came back, his eyes were suspicious, watchful. "What did you do with her?"

He looked bigger to me at that moment, as though he had been pressing weights since I had seen him last—maybe he had given up looking for Lisette and taken up boxing instead, I don't know. Maybe he was armed. Maybe he would attack me and sling my body into a river with a victorious *Ha!* and jump into a car and start driving cross-country in that beautiful tuxedo of his, moonlight glistening in his hair.

I began backing away. "Nothing," I said. "We were friends, that was all. She moved."

He was advancing on me, his face looking sour and even uglier than when we'd first met. How could I have missed the signs before—his physiognomy was all wrong, he had a criminal's face. "So where did she go?"

"I don't know," I said, and retreated so far that the backs of my legs hit the couch and I fell backward onto the seat. I felt something tickling my cheeks and realized I was crying—how undignified. "Go away," I screamed at him, and kicked my legs a little, for good measure. "Go away!"

Perry looked at me disgustedly. "Jesus," he said again, and strode back into the kitchen. When he returned, he was carrying two grocery bags that bulged with mail, which he steadied against his chest as he headed toward the door. As he passed the couch, he paused and looked at me.

"There's something wrong with you," he said. "You need some real help." He kept moving to the door; in another moment he'd be gone.

Something rose up in me then, an agony of bile and anger and frustration. Without having made a decision, I sprang up and found myself running after him and knocked into him with the force of my entire body. His arms were full and he didn't move quickly enough—besides, he didn't see me coming—and he was thrown off his feet and his head hit the corner of the radiator with a thud, louder than you would believe, and he fell to the ground with a kind of grunt.

For a while I lay on the floor where I had fallen as well, my legs tangled in his, aghast, embarrassed. The violence of it was abhorrent. I didn't know what had come over me. "I'm sorry," I said out loud. In a few minutes, when I had recovered myself, I sat up and bent over him solicitously. "I'm sorry," I said again. "Can I get you something to drink?"

He was still, very still. It occurred to me that he hadn't moved at all. "Come on, get up," I said.

He didn't move. He didn't move and he didn't move and he didn't move. Whenever I think back to the scene my stomach curls and my body seizes up, and I am wracked with guilt and all I can think of is *I'm sorry I'm sorry I'm sorry.*

Then again, sometimes I lie awake here at night to the sound of water dripping from the pipes and I get angry, too. I think of Lisette's look of impatience just before she left and how she never called. I think of Perry driving his car at high speeds through Abu Dhabi, a steady beeping emanating from somewhere in the back. I picture Lisette's mail scattered around his body after he'd fallen in a slick litter, catalogs and circulars, dozens of envelopes containing letters and bills and statements disclosing the motions of her new life. I get angry and I think, *We all spend our lives looking for someone; why should he be the one to find her?*

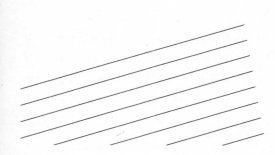

SHANGHAI MURMUR

THE MAN WHO LIVED UPSTAIRS HAD DIED AND IT HAD TAKEN THE OTHER TENANTS DAYS TO NO-TICE, DAYS IN WHICH THE SWEETLY PUTRID SCENT THICKENED AND RESIDENTS TRIED TO AVOID HIS PART OF THE HALL, PALMS TENTING THEIR NOSES AS THEY CAME AND LEFT. At last someone sent for the building's manager, who summoned his unemployed cousin to break the lock and paid him 100 yuan to carry the body down the three flights of stairs.

There was a squabble as the residents who inhabited the adjoining rooms argued that they should have their rent lowered; the death was bad luck. Xiaolei stood, listening, as the building manager shouted them down. She felt sorry for the man who had died, whom she recalled as a middle-aged man with tired, deep-set eyes, who'd chain-smoked and worked at the local post office. She supposed if she ever asphyxiated or was stabbed overnight, the same thing would happen to her.

That evening, she brought back a white chrysanthemum and went upstairs in the dark, intending to leave it outside his room. As she carefully mounted the steps, though, she saw the door stood open. The room was windowless, with a blackness even denser than that of the hall. She didn't wait for her eyes to adjust. She pitched the flower into the void, barely breathing, and ran back down the stairs.

If she came to the store more often, Yongjie would have noticed in a flash the flower was gone; she had the sharp female eyes of a southerner. But most days she wasn't around; in addition to the flower shop, she ran her uncle's poultry slaughterhouse, which occupied most of her time. Since she'd been at the job, Xiaolei probably could have gotten away with taking whole sheaves of flowers: high-waisted, frilly-leaved stems of alstroemeria, clusters of lilac batons. She thought they looked better in isolation, though, and kept her windowsill lined with individually pilfered stems, each housed in its own soda bottle: a tousled-headed rose, a single agapanthus in electric blue.

It had been three years since she'd said goodbye to her parents, telling them she'd gotten a job at a microchip factory down south in Shanghai. Plenty of girls had already left their village; no one expected them to farm anymore. As it happened, she didn't know what a microchip was, but she'd heard a segment about them on the radio. She was sixteen and took a teenager's cruel pride in telling her parents about the microchips — a Japanese company, she'd said authoritatively, that made exports for Europe — and they'd been impressed enough to let her go. All the way up until she boarded the train, she'd been expecting them to catch her in the lie. When they hadn't, she felt disappointed and unexpectedly sad, boarding a train to a city fourteen hours south where she knew no one and had only a phony job waiting.

The next morning, when she got to the flower shop, she was in a foul temper. She had not brushed her hair, and her reflection in the mirror behind the counter made her wince. It seemed that days of fighting to board buses, hustling for space on the sidewalk, elbows always out, eyes half squinted, trying to see if someone was cheating her, lips pursed and ready to answer back, had left an indelible mark. She was not yet twenty but felt the years deep beneath her skin, as though Shanghai had grafted steel plates in her cheeks. Already she'd lost a teenager's mobility of features, felt the exhausted cast of her eyes. Everyone she met had a story about someone from their hometown who'd made it big in Shanghai. Somehow she'd never actually met any of those people firsthand.

Still, she thought, the flower shop had helped. When working at the bottling plant, she'd felt herself turning into something nearly savage, fingers stiff, mind numb, chest a cage. There'd been cats in their village who'd hiss and spit at anyone who came near them, and Xiaolei thought she could understand why. Sometimes if she

wanted to leave her room, she first found herself listening from inside for any hall noises and waiting until they subsided before ex-
iting; the sound of another door rasping open would prompt her
to pause. If she spotted people her age clustered in the courtyard
—a few girls had made friendly overtures—she'd turn and make
a hasty retreat, as if suddenly remembering something. It wasn't
surprising, she told herself: all wild animals fear human contact.

But for six months now, she'd stripped rose thorns and sold
bouquets, and there was a civility to it, an aperture onto a part of
Shanghai that she'd almost stopped hoping she'd ever see, which
soothed some of the growling in her chest. She sold flowers to office secretaries and grieving widows who arrived in sleek black cars
and men who dispatched identical bouquets to separate addresses,
their wives and their mistresses. She learned to flatten her tones
and inflect her voice with a certain inquisitive softness that wasn't
native to any one place, certainly not Shanghai, and customers
seemed to appreciate it.

Her moods were all over the place these days, low currents that
eddied peaceably before surging up into the sand, erasing everything in their path. Maybe someday she'd open her own flower
shop. There were skyscrapers rising everywhere across Shanghai, a
neon tangle of signs and burnished steel, men in suits and women
in high heels, *click click clack*. She could sell potted plants for their
hallways, build up her own business, maybe meet someone in the
elevator, get an office job. It wasn't impossible.

By lunch she had stopped thinking about the dead man and her
spirits began to lift. Outside, the sunlight reflected off the white
strips of the crosswalk, and the street almost glowed. She'd sold six

bunches of daisies that morning and taken in an order for a funeral spray of chrysanthemums; Yongjie would be pleased.

It was Wednesday, so she'd been saving the best flowers all day for her favorite customer, first selling the ones with edges threatening to turn brown, those petals that had started to swoon and go loose at the tips — another two days and they'd come undone.

By five o'clock he still hadn't arrived, though, and she felt a creeping sadness clot her limbs. As she helped other customers, she kept one eye out the door for his silhouette. The light outside was turning that pallid gray of late afternoon, stealing across the sidewalk, muting even the garish red sign across the way that blared HEALTH PRODUCTS, ADULT PRODUCTS, the jumble of computer cords and pipe fittings next door and beyond that, the dirty, slovenly floors of a small restaurant named for its chief menu item, Duck Blood Noodle Soup. He wasn't in sight. She stared resignedly at the remaining flowers, fought the urge to tip them from their buckets onto the sidewalk.

The day after the next was a Friday, meaning she'd have to wake up at 3 a.m. to try and beat all the other flower vendors to the wholesale market across town, then spend the next few hours slopping heavy, wet bundles back to the store. It also meant she'd have to wash out the buckets, already rancid with rotting stems, before leaving for the night. The scent of dying stock flowers, their stems soft and mushy in the water, she thought, compared almost unfavorably to that of her neighbor's corpse.

And then, suddenly, the man was outside the store and smiling at her with his crinkled-up eyes. He ducked inside the door as if he were dodging inclement weather, though it wasn't raining, and rolled his shoulders backward, relaxing them. He'd cut his hair, she noticed, and was wearing the same white collared shirt as always; she envisioned his closet lined with whole glowing rows of them.

At the sight of him, she felt the room come into focus again, her face unfreeze. "Seven red roses and three lilies?" she asked, not quite able to meet his eyes, and he nodded. "The nice wrapping, please." She felt a warm thrum in her chest; the ease he carried with him worked on her like a balm, though he rarely said much —indeed, now that she'd memorized his order, there was scarcely any need to speak at all. She stepped toward the buckets with their floral charges, grateful now for their perked-up appearance, and tucked her hair behind her ears.

Gently, she eased each flower from its bucket and started splaying them out in her left hand, a galaxy of rose heads, then carefully threaded the lilies in among them. Once finished, she slid out a sheet of pink paper and one of purple tissue and laid them tenderly atop each other on the worktable. She thought she could feel his gaze on her and moved more slowly, just for the pleasure of drawing out the moment.

Then, with one unsteady hand, she raised the cleaver and brought it down on the flowers' stems. She placed them at the trembling center of the paper and brought its edges together, carefully tying an orange ribbon around the bouquet's middle. They weren't very nicely assembled, far more ragged than she would have liked, and she hoped he couldn't tell. Yongjie made bouquets perfectly, so even across their tops that you could drape a cloth over them and mistake them for pedestals. She handled all their big orders.

When she turned to look at him, he was standing at the counter, back to her, but as though sensing her movement, turned to look at her expectantly. She could feel little trickles of thought bubbling up that she wanted to share with him, but tamped them down as she handed him the flowers, feeling a jolt as he took them, as though they were an extension of her fingertips. It was foolish, she knew: the flowers were likely for a wife, or a mistress.

"What do you do, anyway?" she said hastily, trying to cover her embarrassment as she assumed her position again behind the counter. "I see so much of you, I've always wondered." That was an understatement; in her mind she'd already constructed an elaborate life for him. He was a doctor specializing in the brain, he played the violin, he liked stinky tofu and walks in the park, had been to Japan.

He looked at her and smiled and the clean lines of his shirt, the dark thatch of his hair, the contrast of it, made her ache. She wanted to lean over the counter and stare at each strand of hair, count the hair follicles on his chin. "I do sales," he said. Then, examining her, as though rethinking his statement: "Well, I'm in sales," he corrected himself, and there was that smile again. He laid the flowers carefully crosswise atop the counter and began fishing for his wallet. "Here, I'll give you my card."

Xiaolei looked down and studied it—it was matte and thick to the touch. The company wasn't one she'd ever heard of; she couldn't tell what they did and she wouldn't insult him by asking.

Outside you could tell the time by the ranks of red taillights forming on the street; dusk was pressing in. Farther down the road was an expensive residential compound sealed with fat shrubs and a tall iron fence around its perimeter. The building, which bore the name Triumph Mansion, was six years old but still had the bewildered air of a fresh transplant; the neighborhood had not yet developed to match the pocketbooks or aspirations of its new residents. Xiaolei looked toward it now, as if for clues. Was she being rude by not speaking? Should she speak?

His gaze was no longer upon her as he fumbled, emptying his pockets, looking for his wallet. The silence had gone on too long. "It's a nice neighborhood," she said hesitatingly at last. "Do you live at Triumph Mansion?"

He looked at her again, longer this time, and his brow furrowed slightly. "I do," he said, and handed her some bills. "Do you?" This, of course, was sheer politesse; she was wearing a smock, it was unlikely a worker like her could afford it, and she could see this same embarrassed realization cross his face as she shook her head and tried to think of what else to say. "A little farther out," she said. He nodded absently, checked his watch.

Desperation surged inside her; she'd already demanded more of him in two minutes than she had in two months. In another moment he'd be gone, would disappear for another week. She counted out his change more deliberately than usual, willing him to ask her a question, any question. He didn't. She paused. "Well, take care," she said, unable to keep the regret from her voice.

He smiled and picked up the bundle of flowers and inhaled. "Thank you," he said, and "See you."

After he left, she started sweeping the green scraps off the table with a wedge of newspaper, flushed around the cheeks, angry with herself. He'd thought her odd, surely, to be asking such questions. Maybe he wouldn't even come back. Asking about Triumph Mansion must have sounded to him so aggressive and strange; she'd been greedy, should have left that question for another week, spaced out all the things she wanted to know, but then that would take months, years, and she didn't want to be at this job that long.

Later on, while helping another customer, she noticed a pen that had been left on the counter. It was black and thick-waisted with a narrow band of silver around its middle and a matching silver clip, a jagged white line on it depicting a mountain. She uncapped it and drew a long stroke against the back of a receipt — its ink was black and dense and flowed under her touch like a thin, controlled river. It must have been his, she thought to herself automatically, and dropped it into her pocket, where it landed with surprising weight.

For another hour between the last two customers (no purchases), she filled out bouquets with the last salvageable flowers; they might sell more quickly that way the next day. As the cars thinned outside, she mixed bleach and water and was on her knees scrubbing out buckets on the sidewalk when she saw a woman stride past her into the store. After a moment, Xiaolei followed her, patting her hands dry on her smock.

Her first impression: big sunglasses with crystal-studded hinges resting on her head, and below that a makeup-free face, so flawless that Xiaolei couldn't stop staring, trying to seek out any imperfection. She had on a pair of snug sweatpants and a pink purse that swung from a strap of golden chains. A soon-to-be bride, she thought, though surprising that she'd come alone and so late. A wife asking where else flowers had been sent, perhaps; it had happened once before.

"My husband left his pen here," the woman said, upon seeing her. "Have you seen it?"

A confusion of emotions flitted across Xiaolei's face like quick-moving clouds. She didn't know what she'd expected the man's wife to look like, somehow not like this, but mentally she paid the woman tribute; she was beautiful, what he deserved, though frankly (Xiaolei thought to herself) there was something off-putting in her face. She looked like the sort of woman who would feed a pet expensive dog food and dock her servants' pay.

An interval passed before Xiaolei realized the silence had gone on too long. "We have some pens," she said slowly, feeling heavy and shapeless in her smock. She went to the cash drawer and brought out a handful of ballpoint pens and laid them on the counter with ceremony.

The woman shook her head, frustrated. "No, I'm talking about a nice pen," she said. "Black, thick," she said, and then she named the brand, which Xiaolei had never heard of. "You must have seen it."

She raised her eyes to Xiaolei's and held them. It was like being trapped in a cobra's gaze: after a minute, just to put an end to it, Xiaolei drew the pen unwillingly from her pocket.

The woman's face struggled between relief and annoyance that it had taken her so long. Relief won out. "Yes, that's the one," she said, and reached to take the pen. "Thank you. It's worth a lot."

Panic seized Xiaolei, irrational and strong, and she pulled the pen back, just as quickly. She put on her best functionary's voice, a mixture of boredom and witlessness. "I'm sorry. I can't let you take it. I can only give it back to the pen's owner."

"I'm his wife," the woman said, face now suspicious.

"Do you have ID?" Xiaolei said.

"Does that pen have ID?" the woman said. "What kind of question is that?"

Xiaolei shrugged.

"Look, it was an expensive pen, a gift from his boss. You wouldn't want to get him into trouble, would you?" the woman said. "If I come back without it, he'll be unhappy, and I'll be unhappy."

Xiaolei stiffened. Then the woman smiled again, such a confident look, and that sealed it. She would not give the woman this pen, no indeed. There was no protocol for expensive lost pens, but if there was, Xiaolei was certain she was in the right; surely one should only return the lost item to its owner. She sat down deliberately at her stool behind the counter, as though to cement her position.

The woman stared at her. "Are you deaf? Give me the pen!"

A couple was passing by outside, an elderly pair of retirees walking in that slow, stooped way of older couples. She knew them by sight; the man used to walk a songbird in a cage by the shop in the mornings until one day he was alone, and she wondered what had become of the bird. On hearing the woman's raised voice, they stopped and looked quizzically at the scene.

The woman made as though to go behind the counter. "Give it to me!"

"No, and you need to stay in front of the counter!" Xiaolei's reflexes were honed after years of living in the city; her right leg shot out and quickly blocked her.

"Thief! Thief!" the woman shouted. "I'll report you to the police!"

Xiaolei was full of indignant fire now; she had what she needed to keep fighting all day. "Go ahead! I'm not going to violate protocol! We have rules," she said proudly.

Seeing the retirees hesitating at the doorway, Xiaolei quickly recruited them. "She wants me to just give it to her, but I can't—there are policies." The elderly woman seemed confused, but after hearing Xiaolei's explanation the man turned to the woman inside and spoke gently. "These policies are for your own protection," he said. "Who would want their lost things to be given away so casually? Tell your husband, tell your husband to come back to the store and get it himself."

At this the woman turned tail and spit on the floor. "You'll be sorry," she said to Xiaolei, and walked out.

Years later, lying awake in bed at night, Xiaolei sometimes thought of all the things she could have done differently. She could have handed back the pen, submitted to the woman, seen her husband the week following and pretended nothing had happened, continued to sell him flowers for weeks and months, an avalanche of roses, an eternity of lilies. She could have held on to the pen and returned it to the husband the following week, or the following day; probably he would have come back in person if it had been truly necessary. She could have kept it in her pocket and never returned to the store, perhaps pawned the pen. Used the money to start her own business.

Instead, after the woman left, Xiaolei closed up the shop in a hurry; she didn't want to risk her returning with the police. She took the pen with her, tucked inside her purse, and rode two buses to a night market, where she sat on a stool amid other workers finished with their shifts and ate a bowl of especially good noodle soup with pickled vegetables, then walked back in the direction of her rented room.

That night she slept poorly, dreaming of the man who had died above her. In her dream, they were riding the same bus in the dark, the brightly lit buildings of Shanghai flashing by in a blur. He was seated a row behind her and leaning forward, his voice a steady, urgent murmur in her ear, the sound of it not unpleasant. He held a bundle of daisies, with petals that tickled her neck. Afterward, the scene shifted, and they were whirling together on a dance floor lit up in an enormous, multicolored grid.

The next day was Xiaolei's day off. Usually she might lie in bed reading dime novels, or occasionally she'd go to the Bund, an hour's bus ride away and one of the few destinations she knew. She liked to gaze across the water at the gleaming pink orbs of the Pearl Tower, and the colored jets of light that illuminated the skyline. Sometimes she sat there for hours, long enough to see the skyscraper lights wink off, just before midnight. Her first year in Shanghai she went frequently, until she overheard a beautifully clad woman telling a friend it was where all the "country bumpkins went to stare." After that, she didn't go so often.

Xiaolei remained in bed awhile, trying to go back to sleep, until at last she rose, feeling restless. She put on a white hooded sweatshirt edged in gold trim that read SUPERSTAR, which she seldom wore for fear of getting it dirty. She donned a matching baseball cap as well, and her nicest pair of jeans. Under her bed she located a tube of bright-red lipstick, which she'd bought shortly after moving to the city. She'd worn it only once before wiping it off, ashamed and startled at the change in her appearance. Today she carefully smeared it across her lips. She shouldered her purse and walked toward the bus, humming softly.

When she'd first arrived in Shanghai, the girls at the bottling plant said there were two ways to make it: get rich or get married. But here she was, still working for a pittance, and the only man to make a pass at her had been her boss at the plant, who was married and three times her age. One day after she'd been there two years, he'd called her in to give her that week's pay. As she bent over his desk to sign the receipt, he leaned against her and squeezed her chest, as though testing the firmness of fruit at a market. "Do you like this?" he'd said, breath hot against her ear. Xiaolei had wrenched herself away and quit not long after, but occasionally found herself wondering whether life would have been better if she hadn't refused him.

She got off the bus not far from Triumph Mansion. As she approached its thick shrubs, she walked more slowly, heart jumping. Its big black gate was locked, but she loitered until she saw another resident leaving, and quickly slipped inside. It was easier than she'd imagined.

Inside it was an oasis, with shrubs clipped into spheres and a marble lobby that contained a golden statue of a trident-bearing angel. The air was perfumed, and from somewhere overhead, a melody was playing, pianissimo. A somnolent guard sat at a front desk, but his head snapped up on seeing Xiaolei.

"Sign in," he grunted.

"I'm just waiting for a friend," Xiaolei said, and ran one hand carelessly through her hair, a gesture borrowed from the man's wife. The guard looked at her hard but didn't say anything.

There was a big mirror on one side of the lobby, and a white leather bench opposite, which Xiaolei sank gratefully into. She took out the pen and gazed at it briefly before slipping it self-consciously back in her bag. The man would thank her for returning the precious item. He would offer her cookies made from paper-thin crepes baked in tight scrolls, and tea served in fragile glassware. Back in the village, when she was not yet a teenager, she had watched a popular television show that depicted the lives of two women living in a big-city apartment upholstered entirely in white—white leather couch, white tufted rug, white lilies—and she pictured his apartment like that, too. They would sit beside each other on the couch. He would press against her like her boss from the bottling plant, only this time, she would not resist.

Hours passed. The air was cool and conditioned, and carried its own kind of quiet hush. A few men in suits and nannies with their beautifully dressed charges came and went. The security guard left and another took his place. Every now and then, Xiaolei pretended to be on the phone, but mostly she just sat and watched the scene. She felt perfectly content there, a thousand miles from the dusty village where she'd been raised, as comfortable as if she belonged. She liked observing the residents' faces, so intelligent and refined, no doubt full of more clever things to say than just *going to rain; guess so; have you eaten yet; yes, hot out today.*

She thought back to her grandfather's eightieth birthday celebration, the year before he died. A big crowd of villagers had assembled for roast fowl, and after a long string of toasts, he'd told them how glad he was that he'd lived all his life among them. He meant it with pride, the fact that he'd never left, but the thought had filled a teenage Xiaolei with horror, and she'd vowed to get away.

A ding from the elevator interrupted her reverie. When she looked up, her favorite customer was disappearing into the elevator, briefcase tucked neatly under one arm. She rose to follow, trying to look casual, but the elevator doors had already slid shut. The gold numbered panel overhead showed him getting off at the fourth floor. Up front, the guard was busy chatting with another resident. In a flash she was hurrying up the stairs in pursuit.

She arrived just as he'd reached an apartment at the end of the hall and shut the door behind him. The floors here were carpeted in dark blue, with faux crystal lamps above. She walked slowly. It was very quiet. There was a mirror by the elevator, and she inspected her face carefully. She removed the baseball cap and wet her lips and smoothed her hair. *You've come this far,* she told herself. *Don't be afraid.*

A few minutes later she was knocking at his door, but there was no answer. After a long while she knocked again, more loudly this time, and heard footsteps. When the door opened, he was standing there in an undershirt and shorts, as though he'd just been changing. "Yes?" he said impatiently. "Who are you?"

Xiaolei tried to find her voice amid her surprise. "I'm —"

"What do you want?" he said. No flicker of recognition registered in his eyes.

Xiaolei heard a woman's voice from somewhere deeper in the apartment. "I don't know," he called over his shoulder. He looked at Xiaolei again, more quizzically this time. "We're not interested."

Inside, she could see a polished mahogany coffee table and a miniature fountain built into one wall that bubbled over a polished black orb. At the sight of Xiaolei, a white poodle curled on the couch stood and barked. The man still didn't appear to recognize her.

"I'm sorry," she said, disappointment crashing over her in heavy waves. She began backing away.

The man eyed her strangely. "That's okay," he said, and shut the door with a click.

Somehow, Xiaolei found her way out of the apartment building, cheeks burning, looking neither left nor right as she hurried down the stairs. Outside, the cool air was a relief. She was sweating profusely, and remembered just in time to strip off her white sweatshirt to keep it from getting stained. It was foolish of her to have gone. It was foolish of her to expect anything of him, to think someone like her might have made an impression on him in any way. She pinched herself hard as punishment, leaving ugly red marks on her arm. She rode the bus and walked home in a daze; once back, she crawled immediately under the covers and lay there, a pit in her stomach and shame in her chest, until she fell asleep.

It was only the next day, after four hours' trundling through the wholesale market in streets slicked with water and dawn half-light, after arriving back at the store to find Yongjie waiting there with an ominous expression, that she'd looked inside her purse and realized the pen was gone. She didn't know if it had been stolen or perhaps slipped out. Anyway, it didn't matter. The wife had found her boss early the previous morning. By the time Xiaolei returned to the shop the following day, arms sopping with bundles of flowers, Yongjie had made up her mind; she was fired. There were plenty of other young girls who could do the job, and probably better, besides.

When Xiaolei heard the amount of money the woman claimed the pen was worth, it astounded her; it was nearly twenty times her monthly salary.

"She must be lying," she said desperately. "What pen costs that much?"

Yongjie hadn't heard of such a pen before, either, Xiaolei was nearly sure of it, but she affected an instant sense of knowingness that came down like a shield. It was a famous European brand, she said.

"Well, then it was probably fake," Xiaolei said, feeling only briefly disloyal. "Who carries a pen like that around?"

Yongjie didn't disagree, but she also refused to pay any of the two weeks' back wages Xiaolei was owed. "You've caused me that much trouble — count yourself lucky it isn't worse," she said. "Word will get around. Triumph Mansion is our key clientele, and now no one will want to come here."

Xiaolei didn't bother to argue; Yongjie probably had a point. At the very least, she'd lost them one of their steadiest weekly customers. "I really did lose it," she said, meaning the pen, but her boss wasn't moved.

"You know it doesn't make a difference," Yongjie said. She was poking white chrysanthemums into a stand of green foam, as if Xiaolei had already disappeared.

In the months to come, as she looked for another job, Xiaolei found herself stopping into the city's small stationery stores seeking out its likeness, wondering if such an expensive pen could possibly exist, and if so, where to find it. She saw thin-stemmed ballpoints and some with outlandish pink and green inks; all kinds of imports were coming in now from South Korea, transparent ones and gel-tips and retractables. She'd hold them in her hands, evaluating them, weighing their worth.

Her only regret was that she hadn't spent more time with the man's pen, cradling it, uncapping it, testing it out for herself, and that she hadn't been able to keep it. She'd gone back to retrace her steps, of course, even interrogated some vendors at the wholesale market, gone back to check the perimeter of Triumph Mansion, but found nothing.

Even when she got another job, this time selling shampoo and conditioner door-to-door, the pen still haunted her. She'd bought a bicycle by then and would ride it up and down the length of the city, leaping off occasionally at stationery stores to check their racks in different seasons. It was a benign quest that gave her some control over a city that otherwise threatened to wear her down.

Once, at a pharmacist's, she saw a woman filling out a receipt with a fat black pen. Its shape was familiar, and her heart stopped. "May I try?"

The clerk knitted her brows, but Xiaolei was sheepish and insistent, and at last she shrugged and gave her the pen and a piece of thin gray cardboard, the inside of a pillbox, to try it on. It was lighter in the hand than Xiaolei had remembered, and had no silver clip, no alpine etching. But it sat in her hand the same way, and it, too, had that glossy sheen. "How much?" she'd asked the woman.

The clerk frowned. "Not for sale," she said.

"Please," Xiaolei said. She started writing with it. It wasn't a fountain pen, she discovered; inside was a raspy ballpoint that skidded over the cardboard's surface, leaving only a wisp of an imprint behind.

"It works better on the pad," the clerk said, and that was true. Xiaolei could see the receipt she'd just written out in a clear black hand. The clerk looked at her curiously, and then pushed the pad forward kindly. "You can try."

But Xiaolei had already disappeared out the door, shaking her head. "Thanks," she called out behind her. "It's not what I'm looking for."

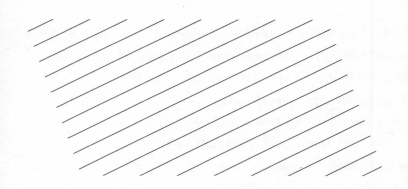

LAND OF
BIG NUMBERS

IT WAS A SCREENSHOT OF A CONVERSATION SENT TO HIM BY LI XUESHI, ONE THAT PROMISED RICHES AND REDEMPTION. *Shandong Abundant Sanitation Ltd. They're going to win a government contract to build six military hospitals,* it read. *Hard-to-come-by opportunity.* The avatars of the two chatting were still visible — a Japanese anime character, a cartoon rabbit — but their names had been blacked out.

Zhu Feng felt his pulse race, as though the little cone of privacy around him and his phone shimmered slightly. *Who is this guy?* he messaged Li. He'd known Li since he was four and they'd lived in the same crummy apartment building; they were almost like brothers.

Don't know. Saw it appear in a friend's timeline. Not a bad tip.

Zhu Feng winced and readjusted his pillow, sprawling on his back. Through his room's cardboard-thin walls, he could hear the sound of his mother chopping in the kitchen and the canned laughter from one of his father's television programs. *Sure, if you have money,* he wrote.

Ask your parents, Li replied. *Better move fast, or you'll miss this one, too.*

God, Li was a lucky bastard. They'd grown up in the same dingy high-rise, with its dirty concrete corridors and busted elevator, but a decade ago Li's father had changed jobs and gone into real estate. He'd moved the family to a complex across town and now ferried them around in a sleek black Mercedes. Li got a "play money" allowance and these days talked constantly of new investments, futures, options — impossible words that sounded to Zhu Feng like exotic forms of freedom. Already his father had promised to buy Li and his girlfriend an apartment whenever they got married.

And then there was Zhu Feng, who still woke every morning in his childhood bedroom. The once-fresh curtains were stained, the bedsheets damp in the humidity. What girl would ever want to marry him, with his joke of a salary, no car, no prospect of a place of his own?

With a sudden flash of determination, he rose and walked into the living room. "Dad," he said brusquely, "I need to borrow some money."

Boyang's rheumy eyes turned from the television and wavered on him. Zhu Feng looked away: something about eye contact with his father made him feel deeply uncomfortable. For a moment, he regretted having said anything at all, but Boyang was scrutinizing him with a furrowed brow. "What for?"

"An investment opportunity. A stock. Li Xueshi said —"

"What does Li know?"

"His family is connected, he knows things . . ."

His father turned his eyes back to the screen. "You have a steady job. If your friend wants to gamble, let him."

"But Dad —"

It was too late. Boyang was already uncapping a tiny bottle of cheap grain liquor and sipping it, as though to fortify himself against his son's words. "The rich don't know what poverty means," he said ponderously, and turned up the volume.

Later, over a dinner of weak beer and lamb skewers, Li was sympathetic.

"The older generation, they don't get it," he said, crunching a deep-fried peanut. For months, Li and another friend had been working to develop an app, one that would let you transpose your face onto a dog, a pig, a Qing emperor, blue tassels hanging down from a square yellow cap. The dog could bark, the Qing emperor could tell you, *May all your wishes come true.*

"There's a whole world out there," Li said. "I keep telling my dad he should back us. He says, 'If I can't hold it, screw it, or eat it, it's not real.'"

Li sighed emphatically, then grinned. "Hey, did I tell you about last night?" He started talking about the latest club he'd taken his girlfriend to, where the alcohol had been served in giant bowls made of ice and the waitstaff all wore glittery makeup.

Zhu Feng nodded along, only half listening, feeling nervous despite himself. When he finally spoke, his voice sounded squeaky and unnatural: "Li, can I borrow some money?"

His friend raised his eyebrows.

"Not much," Zhu Feng hastened to add. "Just a thousand yuan, enough to buy some of that stock you mentioned." He smiled sheepishly as his friend clapped him on his back.

"Anything for you, brother. I never thought you'd get the nerve," Li said. Even before his father had gotten rich, Li had always been the bolder one, throwing spitballs at girls in class, taking more than his portion at school lunches, and talking back to teachers, as Zhu Feng watched self-consciously, envious of his daring.

On the bus back to his parents' apartment that night, riding through the darkened city, Zhu Feng downloaded a trading app. *Do you want to build a new high-prosperity life for yourself?* it asked. He clicked *Yes,* jubilant, and the app installed.

Weeks later, he paid Li back, slapping a pile of red 100-yuan bills onto the white tablecloth of a recently opened five-star seafood restaurant. Together, they toasted with white porcelain teacups that sparkled with newness. The waitresses, with red aprons tied neatly around their backs, were especially pretty, he thought. Shandong Abundant Sanitation Ltd. had done well, doubling in a matter of days after his purchase. On Li's advice, he'd used the money to buy more stock — and that had gone up as well.

The stock market! It was like discovering a secret passcode. It was such easy money. It was a whole *thing* that existed, that minted millions of fortunes all around the country, and now he was finally inside of it. The government was encouraging everyone, too. In one corner of the restaurant, the television was tuned to the state broadcaster and showing the Shanghai index, up 30 percent for the year. "The bull run has only just begun," the anchor was saying. There were hairdressers made millionaires. There were schoolteachers who quit their jobs overnight. THE WORLD'S BEST-PERFORMING STOCK MARKET, another state-run financial daily had proclaimed that morning.

All around Zhu Feng, it seemed, people were buying, buying, homes and stocks and second and third houses; there was a whole generation who'd gotten rich and needed to buy things for their kids, and the same dinky things from before didn't pass muster: penny rides on those plastic cartoon figures that flashed lights and gently rocked back and forth outside of drugstores; hawthorn impaled on sticks and sheathed in frozen yellow sugar casings, a cheap winter treat. They needed to buy because they had the money and that's what everyone else was doing; they had simple lives, and it was their children who were going on to do the complicated things. Also, the government said it was the *buying opportunity of a generation,* everything under construction, new apartments and roads everywhere, China was going up and up and nobody wanted to be left behind.

Even the government office where he worked was being renovated and expanded, new particleboard and conference rooms being added. As the weeks went by and construction dragged on, his coworkers groused at the fumes, but Zhu Feng, glued to his trading app, didn't mind. Everything was poisonous anyway, he reasoned, no matter the quarter of the city you were in; either it was the smog or it was that sickly sweet smell, sharp and chemical, that meant you were near a construction site, some kind of glue, some sort of sealant. You could quail and buy a face mask like so many people were doing now, or you could be a man and just breathe it all in. Pow!

At night, as he lay in bed, he could picture all the stock codes lined up in his head, nodding and waving and flickering in a row. There was 921015, the digits of his birthday. There was 814036, the hog company he'd heard about on the news. There was 640007, another tip from a coworker. He felt tenderly toward them and urged them on, smoke signals spiraling up into the sky.

It wasn't something, he thought, that men like his father could ever understand. Poor men working their poor-men jobs, shut out, wearing their rumpled, baggy old men's jackets, relics of another era, going nowhere. You had to feel sorry for them, really.

For as long as Zhu Feng could remember, his father had been moody, fitful, prone to periods of depression. His mother used to say his father had once suffered a "blow" many years ago, but who hadn't suffered a blow?

"What kind of blow?" he'd ask, on those days Boyang spent simply lying in bed with the shades drawn. She wouldn't say.

Eventually, Zhu Feng stopped wondering. Whatever it was, he should have gotten over it by now. The man was only fifty-three, but already carried a substantial paunch, face liver-spotted and breath reeking. For years he'd worn the same shabby blue hat and fake leather coat and cruised slowly around town on his scooter saying, "*Modi, modi,*" to passersby, hoping they'd hand him some bills and hop on his bike, "*Modi, modi,*" like he was pushing fake Rolexes or hawking children's socks on the street.

When Zhu Feng was young he'd loved to ride with his father on his scooter — the big wheels, the way its engine could roar! It was like sitting astride a great mechanical beast, the steady vibrato of the engine humming underneath, the reassuring sight of the two handles splayed in his father's grip.

Then, as the city got richer and everyone got their own scooters or cars, it saddened him, the thought of his dad waiting for a sign of recognition, scrimping on fuel and coasting, propelled by his feet as much as he could between passengers. Now that Zhu Feng was a grown man with a job of his own, it made him angry, too. Couldn't he try harder? *"Modi, modi."*

For months now, his father's main preoccupation had been a red-billed pet songbird he'd bought at the bird market; he was endlessly unhooking its cage and refreshing its water dish, urging the bird to do its backflips, trying to make it sing. In the mornings, he'd take the birdcage and walk it to a nearby park, where he'd join a group of elderly men, also with their birds. There they would carefully hang their cages in the trees, and spend hours playing chess and chatting. It was all wrong, Zhu Feng thought. Bird-keeping was an old man's hobby, and his father wasn't old yet.

"It's winter," his father had said at first, explaining why he was driving his scooter only a few days a week. "Business is slow."

But that was four months ago, and now it was April, and the fullness of the month was showing in the trees, which unfurled themselves tentatively at first and then in a rain of tiny buds that scattered themselves over the sidewalks. And still Boyang was taking his bird for walks, and still he was driving perhaps just three days a week, forcing Zhu Feng's mother, Junling, to pick up more shifts at the hospital despite her bad back. It made Zhu Feng want to scream.

If only he had more money to invest, he thought. Li Xueshi had recently bought a brand-new speaker set, and the two of them spent hours listening to the sounds of rappers paying frantic homage to places they'd never seen, New York, London, São Paulo. They had beautiful women in their beds and the best of everything: Lamborghini, Rolex, Versace. Together, the two of them mouthed the syllables.

No, there wasn't much for men like Zhu Feng here. He had ideas. He had ambition. He had taste. He liked that phrase, *taste*. It was something that belonged, emphatically, to his and Li's generation. Not the shabbiness of his parents' lives, their shuffling steps, the curtailed hopes that seemed to express nothing more than a desire to *chide bao, chuan de nuan* — to be full in the belly, to be warmly clothed.

If only he had more money. He could double it, triple it, in the market. Everything was going up, up, up around him. In a short time he, too, would be on his way.

Then one day, not long after he'd first begun trading, he made a key discovery. There were a dozen government funds he administered, sending allotments all over the province, filling out the same slips of paper in triplicate that left his hands covered in black ink. He had been handling bank transfers for months before he'd accidentally transposed two digits and sent a batch of funds astray.

He'd found out about it only when the Linyang County forestry bureau had called him demanding to know where their allotment was. By then it was six weeks later, and if they hadn't called him up, it was possible no one would ever have noticed.

At first he'd tried moving 1,000 yuan to his account. He let it sit there for a month before moving it back, and no one noticed. Gradually the dawning realization set in. As long as the books added up when they were tallied at the quarter's end, the money, it seemed, was his. And why not? Why let the money sit there, inert, when it could be spent, used, transformed and multiplied? All those disbursements across the province — there were dozens every month, and who was going to notice an extra account getting its share? No one, that's who.

Swagger swagger get that cash, he chanted to himself. *Swagger swagger make a stash.*

He took out 10,000 yuan and doubled it. The next time, he siphoned off 50,000 yuan and made an additional third on top of that. Every week, he watched the new columns of numbers in his account grow. At the end of every quarter, he moved the original sum of money back to the government's account and plowed the profits back into the market. Eight months passed like that, his mind a whirl of giddy arithmetic. In the mornings, as he walked to the subway, passing ranks of old men gambling on the street over their chessboards, he wanted to crow aloud, *Fools! We have better games now.*

He went downtown to the shops that had English signs, big floor-to-ceiling mirrors, and many-syllabled names: Ermenegildo Zegna and Raidy Boer ("step with world fashion"). He bought new coats, new pants, and a set of sturdy leather shoes, and thrilled to their touch. All around him, he suddenly found himself noticing the brands other men wore, the make of their coats, the look of their cuffs. On the street, whenever he saw the insignias he recognized, he felt his heart give a pleased thump.

At night he returned to his parents' apartment complex, where retirees loitered in the courtyard and the surrounding streets sold nothing more exciting than stale cigarettes and tofu. But for the first time, ascending the concrete stairs, he felt a sense of private elation.

He didn't tell anyone what he was doing, not even Li. Wait until he'd made a fortune, and then he'd surprise them all. He'd quit, start his own company, buy a villa somewhere abroad; lots of people these days were buying passports in Spain, in Greece. Li and his girlfriend had recently gone to Rome — he'd seen the photos. He pictured himself somewhere in Europe, in a sunny café. He'd have to learn a new language, of course. He pictured himself opening up his mouth like a baby bird learning how to sing.

A few times a month for work Zhu Feng traveled to some third- or fourth-tier city, the same sprawling affairs with their knockoff fast-food chains, incessantly honking cars, apartment blocks erected only a year or two previously, and, everywhere, scaffolding like hanging vines. He'd liked that part of the job before, a change of scenery, at least, but since he'd begun trading, he found the trips tedious. It meant poor cell-phone reception, long meetings with local cadres about this fertilizer program or that reforesting effort, days of muddy shoes and terrible food.

On one such trip that winter he and his colleagues set out early, first by train and then by car, six of them in a van that drove an hour and a half along a rain-slicked highway and then bumped unsteadily along a rutted road. They were going to meet with a village party committee to discuss reforesting. Zhu Feng kept his hands curled around his phone, periodically hitting *refresh*. The market opened soft, he saw, dropping 3 percent before the signal cut out. It was chilly, and his breath drew fragile circles that expanded and disappeared on the van's window.

They reached the village and piled out of the van around noon, stamping their feet and breathing into their hands. There were rows of brick houses, piles of rain-softened firewood, and at the entrance, a group of shouting villagers.

The group wasn't very impressive, only twenty or so of them, but they had mustered a hand-painted banner that read GIVE US BACK OUR LAND, GIVE US BACK OUR LIFE, and were waving it energetically.

Zhu Feng didn't know what the banner was referencing, but thought he could guess. Along the highway, they'd passed billboards advertising new high-rises that were going up in the area, the same kinds of computer-rendered images of sleek apartment blocks that plastered cities everywhere now; Zhu Feng assumed these villagers were being relocated to make way for their construction.

"We are not the land committee," the head of the local forestry bureau said loudly to the crowd. "We are with the forestry bureau!" He spoke briskly and with an edge of irritation, as though the protesters had received, but neglected to read, the memo.

The crowd murmured, trying to size them up, but the officials were bundled in coats and the villagers didn't seem to know whom to approach. One woman looked like his mother, Zhu Feng thought, something around the eyes. She wore a puffy red coat with a wide-brimmed straw hat wrapped in plastic against the rain.

From deeper within the village, a group of uniformed men emerged and began hurrying toward the crowd, batons swinging from their hips. A few in the crowd shrieked. At their sight, the woman in the straw hat caught Zhu Feng's eye and rushed over, trying to thrust a sheaf of paper into his hands. "Handsome brother," she said. "You're a young person. Young people must have a conscience."

Zhu Feng hesitated. Up close, the woman was older than he'd realized; he could count the coarse individual hairs above her upper lip. He felt himself weaken, and the woman sensed it. "Help us, please, you are a powerful person, the powerful have a duty." She grabbed his arm, a surprisingly strong tug on his jacket's sleeve. He recoiled.

"Let go of me," he said sharply, and she did. The group of officials swept away, and he followed them into the village's party hall without looking back. By the time they left a few hours later, the clouds had lifted and the protesters were gone.

As they drove away, the local forestry bureau head tried to explain. The villagers in the area were like that, always making trouble, he said. They were being compensated for their farmland and given the chance to be among the first to buy into the new development, which would be state-of-the-art: open-plan kitchens, a flower garden, even an on-site kindergarten. "Life will be better," he said. "They'll get used to it, they'll see."

Zhu Feng wasn't listening. Now that they were back on the road, he opened his phone back up and kept compulsively hitting *refresh,* until he got a wisp of signal at last and saw that the market had dropped 6 percent.

His heart pounded disbelievingly. The day before, as well, stocks had fallen, and the day before that. This was the third day of declines, and they'd already more than wiped out his gains for the past two quarters. It didn't make sense. He stared blankly out the window.

The thing was, he told himself, of *course* the market was up and down, of course he knew that — he wasn't stupid. But the government would never let the market drop. It had happened before, three years ago, and people still talked about it. The market had dropped by more than 40 percent and people were panicking and rushing for exits, but then the government had ordered the country's top hundred companies to buy up shares, push, push, push, make the line hold, and it had. No way the market would be allowed to fail. The government was not very good at a lot of things but it was very, very good at ensuring profits.

The problem was time. There were just two more weeks before the books would be tallied at the end of the quarter by Old Lou, who was drunk most afternoons and deficient at the job, but even he would notice if 100,000 yuan was missing. Two more weeks and four of those days were the weekend — okay, ten more days.

Zhu Feng went to the hotel early that evening, telling his

coworkers he would miss dinner — he wasn't feeling well, he said. He fell asleep with the lights on and woke at dawn with a pounding head.

In the morning, he and his colleagues attended a government seminar on soil remediation, held in a drafty conference room with dozens of other officials and trays of dry buns stuffed with red-bean paste, along with cups of faintly metallic tea. The water wasn't hot enough and the leaves were still floating and caught in his teeth. Every few minutes, Zhu Feng checked his phone: the market, he saw, had fallen another 5 percent.

He texted Li. *Are you seeing this?*

At least you don't have much to lose, Li wrote. *My dad is freaking out, ha ha.*

What's happening?

Dunno, Li wrote.

It didn't make sense, Zhu Feng thought desperately. It wasn't possible. He didn't know how it had happened exactly; it was like a horse, plodding and tractable, had abruptly reared up with spike-armed hooves and bared a mouthful of sharp yellow teeth: *I'm coming for you.*

Zhu Feng's phone lit up again a half hour later. It was a message from Li, this time saying a friend of his father's had heard that the market crash was temporary, that the government was going to step in any day now.

So what are you saying?

Sit tight, Li replied. *Don't worry.*

A great feeling of relief flooded him, one that lingered for only a few minutes before anxiety began to nibble. Even if the market recovered, he thought to himself mutinously, he still likely wouldn't make any money. After all this time, months of risk and hope, what a shame. As an official droned on at the front of the room, Zhu Feng saw, the man sitting in front of him had put his head down on the table and was sleeping. Another woman a few seats over was vigorously picking her nose.

Then another thought occurred to Zhu Feng. He got up and left the room and called his friend from the corridor bathroom. "If the government's going to step in, then it's a good buying opportunity," he said, pleased with his insight.

"Maybe," Li said. He sounded barely awake. Zhu Feng figured he'd been up late working on his app.

"I want in," Zhu Feng said decisively. "Lend me some money, brother, will you?"

Li's voice came, a familiar drawl. "Again? How much?"

"Fifteen thousand," Zhu Feng said boldly, holding his breath.

Li snorted.

"Come on," Zhu Feng said. Li wasn't happy, but Zhu Feng, for once, was insistent. Weren't they good friends? Hadn't he paid him back last time? Give a friend a break, just this one favor. Ten thousand, then. He'd pay him back soon. "Not everyone is lucky enough to have a rich dad," he said.

The bitterness that flooded his tone was impossible to mask, and immediately he regretted it. "I'll pay you back," he said.

"Whatever," Li said.

Back in the conference room, his phone half concealed under the table, Zhu Feng waited a few minutes until Li's transfer came through before clicking *buy, buy, buy*. Watching the new stock codes appear on his ticker, he tried to put the conversation with Li out of his mind.

All during the train ride back, Zhu Feng expectantly refreshed his phone, waiting for the market to rebound, but it kept falling. The next day, he ate beef noodle soup for lunch and dinner at the sticky-tabled stall around the corner from his office: beef for cows, beef for bulls, for a bull market. He wore the same pair of lucky red underwear all week and waited for the government to intervene, but every time he opened his app, the market had refused to go back up; it stayed stubbornly low and even fell further.

He'd texted Li, letting him know he was back in town, but received no reply. A few times he began writing a message that read *I thought your dad's friend said,* but stopped himself. He was lonely. At home, his father's pet bird cawed at all hours. Zhu Feng kept to his room with his headphones on.

Around the country, investors were furious, but what could they do? The government papers stopped cheerleading the market, and instead reported its decline with clipped precision on their inside pages. A few ran editorials about overly greedy investors who'd helped drive up prices: *irrational behavior, market rumormongering,* they said, *needs correction.*

For Zhu Feng, time had narrowed to just one point, the small square of calendar that showed the end of the quarter, when the government's books would be tallied. No matter what he did, the days were moving swiftly, inexorably ahead. If the market dropped further, he knew, the sensible thing to do was probably sell, but then what? If he sold, he'd lose any chance at all of recovering his losses, and he was now more than 150,000 yuan down.

He started borrowing small sums of money from people at work, not much, but every penny counted. He'd even tried taking some of his recently purchased clothes back to stores to return, but the shopkeepers just gave him funny looks and shook their heads.

With seven days to go, the market went up slightly, but stumbled again the day after. The morning after that (five days to go), following another sleepless night, he knew it was time to bury his pride. *I'm really sorry, brother,* he wrote Li. *I'm in trouble. Are you there?*

After sending the message, he felt the knot in his stomach relax. Li would be shocked when he confessed what he'd done, was probably still angry after their last exchange, but he'd do his best; he was that kind of friend. It was possible, he told himself, that Li would even approve of the sheer audacity of his scheme. Once, when they were six, they'd stolen 100 yuan out of Li's mother's purse and used it to buy themselves sodas every day for a year, to the envy of their classmates; the memory made Zhu Feng smile.

He lay in bed for another hour, listening to the cheesy sound of slapstick coming through the wall and waiting for Li's reply. It was Saturday and he didn't have to work. He called Li's phone, once, twice, three times, each time getting a swarm of hip-hop in his ear, a ringtone he remembered the two of them buying together the previous summer.

But when Li finally replied, he sounded distracted: he was at the airport with his girlfriend, about to leave for a week's holiday abroad. *Talk to you when I'm back,* he wrote, and that was all.

• • •

Zhu Feng's heart dropped. He tried calling again, but Li's phone was powered off. He got out of bed, limbs feeling like those of a condemned man. He made himself undress and went to take a shower. Standing under its spray, he was flooded with a feeling akin to homesickness and he sat down, letting the water pelt his head.

He was still sitting there, head cradled on his knees, when Junling rapped at the door. "Are you okay?" she called.

"I'm okay."

"I have to go to work," she said.

He turned off the water and dried himself and exited in a cloud of hot steam. His mother was standing there in her scrubs, wincing a little, the way she did in the mornings when her back was especially bad. She pushed her way inside and closed the door.

After Junling left, he decided to go for a walk, anything to get out of the apartment. Outside, he passed the park where his father took his bird; a few of the other men were out already, peering over a chessboard, birdcages hanging in the trees. He passed the old drugstore that had been there since his childhood, with a new sign now, under new ownership. He passed a vegetable stand where retirees were sifting through discounted piles of wilted greens.

He would tell his parents that night, he decided. He would explain what he'd been doing and how he'd lost the government's money, and see what help they could offer. They were his parents, after all.

Every few minutes, he felt the urge to refresh his phone and check on the market, before remembering with relief that it was Saturday, and the markets were closed. He kept walking.

He passed the bus station, a few high-rises, some hairdressing salons, a pet store. He squared his shoulders and continued south. An hour and a half later he hit the downtown, and at first he meant to stop, maybe browse in some of the shops, but instead he pressed on —there was something exhilarating about it; he could walk forever, he felt, his feet barely aware of their exertions. To the west, he could see the white towers of the neighborhood where Li's family now lived, but he kept going straight, cutting across the city toward the hills.

He returned home only after dark. Boyang was in the living room, watching the television as an advertisement for expensive alcohol came on. The bottle was blue and bathed in an eerie light and revolved onscreen as a man's deep voice intoned, "Time-honored quality, Chinese quality."

From the kitchen, Zhu Feng could hear the sound of oil hissing in a pan. His mother was stir-frying slivered potatoes with vinegar on the stove. She was still wearing her scrubs from the hospital, white with yellow trim. It was unusual for her, so much so that Zhu Feng asked if something was wrong.

"Nothing," she said, annoyed. "I was pressed for time tonight. We had people lining up for hours today. We cycled them through in two-minute slots."

Zhu Feng took the garlic without being asked and began peeling. For a nurse his mother had clumsy fingers, and her eyesight had begun to fail; he'd found that if he didn't handle the garlic, bits of the papery scales would wind up in the cooking.

She brushed past him to pick up two pieces of fish that sat on the counter, which she dredged in a plateful of flour. "I didn't know you were eating here tonight," she said, looking down at their limp bodies distastefully, by way of explanation. "You and your father can eat it."

Junling slid the fish into the hot oil of a pan, where they began to sizzle. As he watched, Zhu Feng could see a smudge on one of his mother's sleeves. It looked like some kind of bodily fluid. He shuddered. From the living room, the television blared.

"Did Dad go out today?" he said.

She added a few flecks of red chili to the pan and a sprinkling of ginger and chopped scallions. "Don't know."

"Bet he stayed home."

Her lips tightened as she flipped the fish. "Business is poor," she said. "It was better when he used to drive the taxi."

"He drove a taxi? I don't remember that." For as long as Zhu Feng could recall, his father had been driving the same scooter, *"Modi, modi."*

"Before you were born."

"Why did he stop?"

She was silent. "It was after the incident," she said at last, extracting the fish and laying them in a shallow bowl.

"What incident?" he said.

Junling pretended not to hear him; it was like he was ten all over again, wondering why his father was lying in bed with the shades drawn in the middle of the day.

"Just tell me," he said, exasperated. "What's the big deal, anyway?"

"It was so long ago."

He waited.

"At the time a lot of students were protesting." She began chopping the cabbage, but slowly, as though her mind were elsewhere.

Zhu Feng frowned; it was not what he had expected. "What kind of protests?" He pictured the villagers that previous week: their feeble banner, their stacks of papers, the men with their batons.

The protests were happening all over the country, Junling said. Thousands of students were taking to the streets, talking about democracy, corruption, political reform. A number of taxi drivers joined them, and other workers, too. "A lot of grievances," she said. "Too many rotten government officials."

Zhu Feng remembered he'd heard of something like that happening, long ago; he dimly recalled one history professor alluding to it during class before changing the subject. He strained to remember any other details. "This was in the city?" he asked.

"Yes," she said, ferrying pale handfuls of cabbage to the pan. "It was chaotic. They flipped two police cars. It went on for days; there must have been thousands of protesters."

It was hard to imagine; he'd never seen a protest like that in his life. He wished he could've seen it.

"Dad was involved?"

"He was different then," she said. For a moment she almost smiled. "It was a different era. People were very idealistic. Not like today."

"And then what happened?"

His mother threw the garlic into the pan and added salt. She didn't answer, and he repeated his question. "Ma, I'm not small anymore," he said, and she nodded, as though he'd made a good point.

There were newspaper reports that protesters were armed with knives and explosives. Others said it was just fireworks being set off — the police were mistaken. The crowds kept multiplying: peaceful, but they were bearing all kinds of banners, calling for the vote, for a free press, the crowds fed upon themselves, and soon the police were firing. Boyang had clambered atop one of the tipped-over cars and was brandishing a megaphone at the time. He was hit in the thigh.

Zhu Feng thought he'd heard incorrectly. His father, who spent his days fussing over his pet bird? His father, defeated scooter driver, atop a patrol car, with a megaphone?

"The police said they were warning shots, but three people got hit anyway," Junling said, stirring the cabbage with a spoon. "They said it was an accident."

"Hit?"

"One of them killed."

Zhu Feng didn't know what to say. "So he stopped driving a taxi?"

"They wouldn't license him," she said matter-of-factly. "It took him years to get back on his feet again."

"Anyway, it was a long time ago," she said. Outside the television was playing a commercial for luxury men's cologne.

She extinguished the flame below the pan. "Come on," she said. "Let's eat."

They ate without speaking, the sound of the television noisy in the background. His mother stared at her plate. Boyang, out of the corner of his eye, watched a martial arts fight happening on the screen, heavily stylized, men flying backward in the sky, their crouches and kicks rewound and shown in reverse, knives going backward and landing neatly back in their holsters. A woman clad in gray with her hair in a topknot stood making hysterical noises as they flew around, calling, "Wei-yuan! Wei-yuan!" Zhu Feng knew the show, it was called *Time Clock,* and its central plot involved the fact that, periodically, time moved backward at random intervals, confusing all the characters. It was a stupid show.

He looked uneasily at his father. "Dad," he said, trying to re-call his resolve from earlier that afternoon, "I wondered if I could maybe borrow some money."

His father grunted. "What for?"

Zhu Feng didn't meet his eyes. "It's complicated," he said. He thought of what his mother had said in the kitchen—too many rotten officials—and felt something twist in his chest. Maybe they didn't need to hear the whole story.

"I owe money to a friend," he said.

"Don't you have a job?"

"This was from before," he said.

"What friend?"

"Li Xueshi."

"You shouldn't borrow money from friends. Don't you know how it looks, to have you going around like a beggar?"

"Right, I know I shouldn't have," he said, unable to bear the sus-pense, wanting to get it over with. "So could you—"

His father interrupted him. "How much?"

"One hundred fifty thousand yuan."

Boyang looked genuinely astonished, then laughed without mirth. "Where would I have that much money?" Zhu Feng waited for him to say something further, but that was all.

Junling had dropped her chopsticks with a clatter. "One hundred fifty thousand yuan," she said, and then repeated the sum out loud. She looked at him, and Zhu Feng was struck by the fear on her face. "I don't understand," she said. "How could you owe so much?"

The silence expanded and filled the table. Zhu Feng waited for them to say something else, to offer something, anything, but there was nothing. A hollow feeling was stealing over him: panic, he suspected, was not far behind. "Forget it," he mumbled.

He served himself some more cabbage, trying to camouflage the shaking in his hands. He shouldn't have bothered asking them, he thought resentfully. It was useless to expect anything of them.

After a few more bites, he pushed back his chair and left the table. He went to his room and lay down, trying not to think about what had just occurred. Instead he thought about what his mother had said about Boyang, a story nearly impossible to square with the man who had raised him. He tried to picture his father getting struck in the thigh with a bullet. What had he been thinking? What kind of man had he been then? Angrier, surely, more full of life. He pictured the scene again, only now, like *Time Clock,* the bullets moving backward, out of his father's thigh, his thigh sealing up, the hole in his pants healing, the bullet reversing its trajectory through the sky, back into the barrel that fired it. His father probably still wouldn't be rich. But maybe he'd be strong.

Outside, his mother was clearing dishes with a clatter. He heard the television being silenced, water sounding in the bathroom, and the click of his parents' door as it shut. He turned on his side and pulled the sheet up.

Give it a few more days, he told himself. *Just a few more days and you will be fine.* All that anxious refreshing, all that marking of time — what was the point? He had days to work with, which were made up of hours, made of minutes, made of seconds — he was young, he had time. This was the way the world worked: you couldn't buckle over, couldn't be afraid. Something would step into the breach, he told himself. The market would straighten itself out, the government was going to intervene. The world was a profusion of opportunities waiting to be unfolded, he thought as he drifted off to sleep. He had only to stretch out his hand.

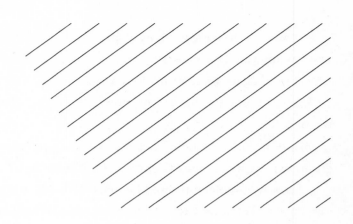

BEAUTIFUL COUNTRY

WE ARE RIDING IN THE CAR WHEN HE SPOTS A SET OF RAMSHACKLE STALLS WITH HAND-PAINTED SIGNS AND PULLS OVER. Eric can't resist the sight of hand-writing trying to sell him things, whether it's a kid's lemonade stand or swirly script on a bistro chalkboard, or in this case, a high-way sign saying NATIVE CRAFTS.

I try to avoid looking too long at any one bracelet but Eric picks one up anyway. "It's genuine turquoise," the woman says, and helps him slide it over my unwilling wrist.

The beads are too bulky, the silver too bright. "I'm okay," I tell him.

"It's beautiful," he says. "Besides, we're supporting the local economy." He hands her a twenty over my protests.

I thank him reluctantly, and he nods. "You like turquoise," he says, so proud of himself for remembering that I briefly forgive him his generosity.

Farther down, a woman is selling dream catchers made from rawhide and feathers. He asks for tips on good local food, and seems disappointed when she recommends a fast-food joint nearby. He asks whether she uses dream catchers herself, and she hesitates before saying yes.

He buys two, one for his mother and one for his sister. And because I feel guilty about my lack of enthusiasm for the bracelet, for this trip, I buy a cheap, postcard-size sand painting I see him eyeing, a crude geometric figure made from pink and beige sand. I don't admire it myself, but I pay the woman and carefully count and fold the bills she hands me into my wallet.

When we get back in the car, he turns to me. "Just so you know, you shouldn't count the change like that in front of someone," he says.

"Why not?" I ask, mystified.

"It's rude," he tells me. My cheeks get hot. Even after more than a decade in this country, I'm still getting caught out.

"It's okay," he says kindly. "You didn't know."

• • •

The sky is lined with furrows of long, heavy clouds as we drive into the park. It's late in the day, yellow panels of light in the trees. I tell him we're probably going to miss the sunset. "There'll be another one tomorrow," I say.

He doesn't answer, but pushes down on the gas. Beneath his happy-go-lucky air, there's a hardness in Eric that doesn't tolerate failure, not in the people he loves, anyway. The night before last, when he got home from work, I greeted him on the couch, still in pajamas, as I'd been all day. It had been a week of extra shifts at the hospital, and I was drained. "You're so crisp," I said, trying to sound cheerful, feeling the starch in his shirt crinkle. "Like a potato chip."

"And you're like a potato," he said, ruffling my hair harder than necessary. "Come on, let's get you out of the house."

The trees at the Grand Canyon are scraggly and shake in the wind. The sun is low and waiting to fall. We park at an outlook and walk toward the edge, hand in hand. The canyon stretches before us, all shadow and orange cliffs and a white finger of river. Eric makes a hoop with his arm and pretends to catch me in it, like a butterfly net, and I pretend to laugh.

Around us are retirees in hats, families with squirming children, and tourists speaking different tongues. I catch a few snips of Mandarin: an SUV of young Chinese travelers has just parked, and I stifle the urge to immediately rush over and say hi. After a day's drive across empty landscapes, the crowds are a relief. *What's the opposite of claustrophobia,* I wonder. *What's the word for feeling you can relax only in a crowd?*

Farther down, a man with a goatee takes out a guitar and plunks away. The instrument is halting, the man's voice rich and creamy and beautiful. I look up to smile at Eric, but he's turned away. "Let's find someplace quieter," he says.

He heads to the side of the lot, where the guardrail ends, and I follow. The earth is burnt orange and craggy. I can see what's caught his eye — a cluster of flat rocks jutting out from a ledge that's fifty feet away and a steep scramble down — and roll my eyes.

"Let's just watch it from here," I say.

"This is better," he says, already four paces ahead.

Not long after we first met, when I was right out of nursing school, he insisted on taking me backpacking. "You'll love it," he told me. He took me to hike a glacier, where I was terrified every few feet it would crack and send me into freezing water. We hiked a forest trail with gnats so thick they got in your eyes. I sent dutiful photos to my parents, like: "Look! Trees! Your daughter in America, enjoying nature's splendors!" Since we moved to Tucson, though, Eric's love of the great outdoors has been mostly a solo affair. Every year or so, he and his buddies will go camp somewhere, Utah or Colorado. "You should come," he'll say. "It'll be good for you." I tell him I've seen trees before.

I follow him now, feeling my legs start to wobble. There's a new chill in the air as the sun retreats, and I wish that I'd brought a jacket.

"The colors are so great," he calls back exuberantly. "They remind me of when we visited this petrified forest as kids." Eric's parents drove a VW Bug cross-country after college, before becoming stockbrokers who occasionally smoked joints with their teenage kids. They were those kinds of parents.

"Did the trees look scared?" I say.

He laughs, and waits for me as I clamber down, gingerly moving sideways.

"See, you're fine," he says.

The sun is a tiny dot of egg yolk, pulling all the brightness in the sky with it as it sinks. We find a shelf of chalky rock to sit on, several feet back from the edge. I take a few deliberate breaths and try not to look down. The wind doesn't reach us here.

He puts his arm around me. "Beautiful, isn't it, pickle?" he whispers with a proprietary glow, and I nod.

From this angle, the canyon is in shadow, nothing like the gas station postcards I bought earlier showing a molten gold vista at sunset, three for a dollar. I tell myself to relax and enjoy the moment. I tell myself this will be the year that Eric gets his promotion, that I will find a better job, and we will get married at last. I tell myself not to be too concerned that I found a lipstick case on the floor of his car last week, one that wasn't mine. In our eight years of dating, Eric has been unfaithful just once, and since then, we've been happy. There are nurses at the hospital who tell me that I'm lucky, they've been in relationships with worse.

"There it goes," he says. It takes me a moment to realize he's talking about the sun.

Back at the outlook, a tour bus has parked and a couple dozen Chinese tourists have descended. They're the kind of tourists I never used to see in the U.S.: older, faces dark and wrinkled like those of migrant workers in large Chinese cities, wearing matching red-and-white hats, flush with newly disposable cash. Farther down, a group of Russians are milling around with big cameras, and a slim-hipped couple with identical platinum hair is kissing by the railing.

We get back in the car and Eric rolls down the windows, letting the scent of sagebrush rush in.

"All the national parks are so crowded now," he says as we drive on. "When we were kids, it was never like this."

I don't say anything.

During a road trip last spring, he says, he and his buddies hit an hour-long traffic jam in Yellowstone, after too many cars stopped to look at bear cubs gamboling in a meadow. "It was ridiculous," he says, shaking his head. "I mean, come on, people, leave them alone."

I think to myself, *I would have been one of the people photographing the bears.* Then, as Eric starts talking about slacklining and free climbs, I look out the window and think about hibernation: how wonderful, to fall asleep and wake up to a new season.

We eat at a crowded diner that serves ice water in glasses as big as boxing gloves and something called a Shark-o-Rama, which the table beside us orders, an electric-blue drink with shark gummies and whipped cream on top.

The waitress doesn't take our orders for so long that I grow impatient and march them over myself, rather than resort to the delicate ballet of eye contact that Eric prefers. "We're in a hurry," I tell her, even though we're not, because I assume otherwise it'll take another hour to get served. I am patient about most things, but not food.

As we eat, Eric tells me about a director at his firm who recently returned from a business trip to China. "His girlfriend wanted a vase from China, but he didn't have time to shop," he said. "So he just bought her one from Pier One when he got back."

"Ha ha," I say.

For our anniversary last year, Eric came with me to visit China for the first time. He charmed my parents with his bad *ni hao*s and brought them gifts of Hershey bars, which no one had the heart to tell him local supermarkets had sold for years. He snapped photos of Chinglish at restaurants and of old men playing chess in the streets. He liked the food but confessed himself disappointed in the Great Wall, which was so crowded with people, he said, that it would've been easier to crowd-surf than climb. "Sorry, I just wanted to be honest," he told me, and I thought to myself, *Sometimes it's okay to lie.*

Like the nurses at my hospital, everyone thought he was so handsome, even as I could sense my parents' skepticism that he had been with their daughter for so long and somehow not proposed. "I hate that you're so good-looking," I once told him after we'd started dating, only partly in jest. "It means you can get away with anything." He didn't argue.

The next morning, we stop at the visitors' center before heading out for a hike. I fill our water bottles and study a sign explaining the differences between sedimentary and metamorphic rocks. Eric gets a map and we drive another mile before parking at a trailhead and setting out. He is whistling as we walk, and the sound of it grates on me.

"Please stop," I say, and he does.

Seen in the thin morning light, the Grand Canyon is a vision of fairy-tale orange and rust and misty blue. The trail we're on follows its rim. It's paved and turns out to be popular with women with strollers and retirees with slow-moving, pendulous rears, which we keep passing. I can sense Eric's determination to overtake them all, and also that it's not going to happen. The trailhead parking lot was packed. I don't know why he's always so fixated on getting Mother Nature by herself, anyway, like he's a guy at a party trying to corner a pretty girl.

For a moment I flash back to my childhood in Dalian, northeast China. On weekends, families would visit the nearby park, with its cheerful stands selling kites and snacks, its shrieking children and litter of peanut shells, and elderly men who would stroll solemnly, equipped with handheld radios blasting high-pitched Chinese opera. Everyone grumbled over the 10-yuan ticket price, but it paid for the park to bring in hundreds of tulips, which they planted every spring. It wasn't natural, but it was nice.

"Maybe we could go back to China this summer," he says, as though reading my mind.

"I'd like that," I say. "My parents are getting older, you know." At night sometimes I lie awake and worry that they'll slip and fall or get into an accident while I am here, so many thousands of miles away. Each time I see them, they are more gray and brittle than the last.

"They're only in their sixties," he says. "Same as mine."

But his parents are the kind of sixty-year-olds who plan hikes on Machu Picchu with other energetic retirees, and dance the rumba at their friends' vow-renewal ceremonies. Mine are the kind who worked in the fields the first thirty years of their lives, and then in a semiconductor factory, fitting tiny parts inside of other tiny parts, until their fingers and backs were crooked. If it weren't for my uncle, who worked for the government, I never would've had the chance to study abroad.

I'm about to tell him that when a trim woman jogs by in tight blue leggings and a magenta top. She has piercing blue eyes and ash-blond hair, and only her skin gives her age away, so finely crinkled it looks like that of a desert turtle. She gives us a quick, accusing stare as we move out of her way, also so turtle-like that we look at each other and stifle a laugh.

"Age is just a number," Eric says.

That night, I call my old friend Jessica, who, even in scrubs, was so statuesque and beautiful that the sound of her voice, deep and throaty like a man's, always caught everyone by surprise. She moved away years ago, and I can hear the sound of Maine in her tone: the warm sweater she's wearing, the fuzzy boots, and the ease that comes with the fact that both her children are asleep, like the two angels they are. My goddaughters. I tell her about the colors here, the way the clouds cast ever-shifting shapes on the landscape, a slow-drifting blue chimera.

"So you're forgiving him," she says.

"There's nothing to forgive," I tell her. "It was just one tube of lipstick."

She says, "The Grand Canyon is beautiful. That doesn't mean he isn't a jerk."

"Relationships are about trust," I say, and wonder at the preachy tone in my voice. It sounds familiar, and then I realize it's borrowed from all the daytime talk shows that I've been watching lately.

We are both quiet. I can picture her frown, the way she's probably tucking the phone against her shoulder as she knits or maybe does a crossword, always busy, getting things done. Eric always liked her. Back when we'd first arrived in Tucson and she was still single, after a rough day we would go out with the other girls on our floor and she would slam down shots and toss her long hair and outdrink everyone in the bar.

"You've been together eight years," she says. "What is he waiting for?"

I think back to the early days after Eric and I first moved in together, the exhilaration of seeing our books lined up on the same shelves, of a shared bag of groceries. Once, during a rainstorm in Tucson, after a new carpet had been delivered to our apartment — the first big thing we'd bought together — we lay on it and talked about our hopes for the future. I told him I pictured children running on grass wearing candy-colored clothes, days spent playing in sandboxes and kindergarten teachers gentle as bunny rabbits. He said that sounded nice.

"He could have given someone a ride home from work," I say.

• • •

After lunch, on our way back south, I tell Eric that the name "America" in Chinese, *Meiguo,* means "beautiful country." When I was very young, I confess to him, I pictured a pastel-tinted land of flowers. On TV shows, I say, the sight of so many Americans who worked ordinary jobs—teachers and handymen—and still lived in enormous houses, with lawns like green moats, astounded me.

"In China, we would've called them villas," I say.

"I know," he says. "You've told me."

He is distracted, scanning the horizon for signs of rain. The air has been getting heavy, the way it does before a storm. Part of me hopes it will pour, flood the roads, a real "weather event," like they say on the news. In Tucson, the flash floods are nearly biblical. One moment, the land is dry as a bone, the saguaros parched and skinny. The next, the rain is lashing down, the sound of an angry god pummeling the city with a thousand tiny stones, and the streets course like rivers. It's the closest thing I've ever seen to an apocalypse, and it's always a wonder, a relief.

Afterward, the waters recede and the saguaros' pleats grow full and disappear. The sun beats down and the land turns orange once more. America is indeed very *mei*—very beautiful—but Arizona, I sometimes tell my friends back home, is like living on Mars.

I look at Eric and wonder what he's thinking, but don't ask. When we first started dating, I'd ask him all the time, and finally he told me to please stop. "I'm an open book," he said. "What you see is what you get." He was that way, too, when I first found out about the woman he'd been seeing a few years ago, a client of his: after I confronted him, he had nodded and said, in just as straightforward a manner, that they had slept together twice and he was very sorry. "I wish it hadn't happened," he'd said matter-of-factly, as though describing something that hadn't actually involved him.

Outside, the rain starts coming down hard and fast. "We should maybe find a place to pull over," he says. It's a narrow two-lane highway, not forgiving for skids. He told me once that his grandmother's parents had both died in separate car crashes, and so he's always been a careful driver, ever since he was a teenager. It's one of the things I like about him, his caution on roads, the safety that comes with him behind the wheel. I tried explaining that to Jessica once, how happy I feel with him when we're together in the car.

"Sure," she said. "It's the feeling that you're moving forward."

When the rain starts pelting down in earnest, we pull over and seek shelter in a huge white roadside structure that says JESUS SAVES CHEAP GAS SOUVENIRS. On one side is a stand with two gas pumps, and inside, a cavernous potpourri-scented shop selling cheap magnets of Arizona license plates with different girls' and boys' names on them and mugs with slogans like TODAY SOMEONE THINKS YOU'RE AWESOME and NO COFFEE, NO WORKEE. There are glass cases of miniature horses and cowboys and natives with feathered headdresses cast in resin, and an inexplicable unicorn or two. There are friendship bracelets and mood rings. Out of habit, I buy a few things to give to family back home, things that will pack well—a Grand Canyon coaster, some magnets shaped like sagebrush—and peel off the tiny gold stickers that say MADE IN CHINA. By the time I make my once-a-year trip to see them, a little motley pile has always accumulated. By now my parents' apartment is covered in the strange flotsam of such tokens from across America.

The woman at the cash register rings me up and clucks appreciatively at my purchases. "I love these," she says, tapping the sagebrush magnets. "Always think they're kind of goofy."

I ask if she's the owner and compliment the stand of trees growing out front that we passed on our way in. "They're lovely," I say, and they are, a tall trio bearing a loose froth of yellow-green leaves, with bark that's green, too.

"It's all the chlorophyll," she says. She tells me she planted them three years ago, along with the flowers out back.

I'm genuinely astonished. "You mean the trees are only three years old?"

She laughs. "Sure. From little bitty seeds."

My reaction seems to amuse her. "It's the Arizona state tree, honey," she tells me. "Paloverde. They grow real fast, and can live to be a hundred years old."

"Where are you from?" she says, and when I reply, she says, "Oh, wow. China. What's that like?"

It was a question that used to throw me, back when I first arrived in the U.S., when I would run through memories of high school and family and then freeze, not knowing what to say. Now I know. "It's far," I say, smiling. "It's very nice. Good food."

Eric comes up from behind and puts his arms around me. "It's been a while since she's lived there," he says. "We live in Tucson now." I know he's trying to make me feel more comfortable, but it also feels like he's interrupting. I like this woman, with her gray hair, green thumb, and mugs with their terrible, well-meaning slogans.

"Gosh, I always thought I'd love to go to China," the woman says. "Never left the state."

"I really like Arizona," I tell her, smiling, and it occurs to me that I do. My parents came to visit once, not long after we'd moved here. I showed them malls and parks and museums, but really what they couldn't get over was the heat and the sun and the big blue sky. As soon as I settle down, they plan to join me.

Overhead, the rain is thundering so hard that we almost have to raise our voices. When it's over, the sky will turn gold, and then purple, a true Arizona sunset. There's a lounge on the seventh floor of our hospital that offers a panoramic vista of the mountains, facing west. Our cancer patients like to visit at sundown, hooked to their IV drips. It's so beautiful that sometimes after treatment they come back to visit, the ones who are well.

By 4 p.m., the number of people taking refuge from the rain has swelled, and soon the woman is busy attending to other customers. She's taken out a plug-in burner and a coffeepot and looks flushed from all the tourists and truckers who've suddenly descended, turning her postcard carousels with slow creaks and peering over rows of painted votive candles. "Oh, my," she keeps saying. "Welcome. What a storm."

I wander in search of Eric, two coffee cups in hand. When I find him, he's retreated to one end of the store, a green-carpeted expanse set up like a small church, with six wooden pews and an empty pulpit. There's a piano in one corner with what look like real ivory keys.

"You disappeared," I say, and edge into one of the pews beside him.

He accepts a coffee cup without looking at me. "We can probably get back on the road soon."

"There's no hurry," I tell him. "The owner has some cookies in the back she says she'll bring out for everyone," I say. "She's so happy for all this company."

The roof slants over this part of the building, and here the rain isn't so loud; it makes a soft, sensuous patter. I spread my fingers over the coffee cup, warming them, and lean my head on Eric's shoulder. His eyes are to the front, as though watching someone deliver a sermon, and he puts his arm around me and absently tweaks a strand of my hair.

"The woman says those trees out front are only three years old," I tell him. "Isn't that amazing?"

He says it is.

We are quiet for a while, listening to the rain. Behind us, I can hear children laughing, and what sounds almost like a party in progress. I peek back toward the counter. A large man with a baseball cap has purchased one of those decorative tins of chili and caramel popcorn, and is loudly urging others to dig in. The woman beside him, his wife, probably, is shaking her head and rolling her eyes. There's a mighty crack of thunder in the distance, and a collective cry from the crowd, an appreciative one, that it is outside and we are in.

I turn back to face the front again. The wood of the pew isn't comfortable, but Eric doesn't seem inclined to move.

"It's been a good trip," I offer at last, wondering if I should ask him about the lipstick.

He nods and kisses my head, then deposits another kiss on one shoulder. The pew has a pile of softcover Bibles stacked in one corner. I imagine quiet Sundays here and the liturgy, the passing of the peace. Sometimes in the oncology ward, I'll offer a few prayers that I learned from the hospital chaplain, and others from patients, too. *God grant me the wisdom to accept the things I cannot change* was one, and for a while I recited it for patients, until someone told me it was a prayer for alcoholics.

I put Eric's hand in mine and study it, and he curls it around my fingers in a warm grip. I have known this man longer than I have known most people, I think. We have shared countless meals and car rides and our toothbrushes have hung side by side for almost a decade. He is weak, I think, but also kind, and tenderhearted, and in moments like these, I tell myself that's enough.

The rain comes down a while longer and then abruptly begins to lift. Just before we stand to leave, Eric gestures toward the front of the small chapel with one movement of his well-cut jaw. "That'll be us someday, pickle," he tells me with satisfaction.

He says it with the air of watching a beautiful sunset on the horizon, and there is only the slightest of pauses before I agree.

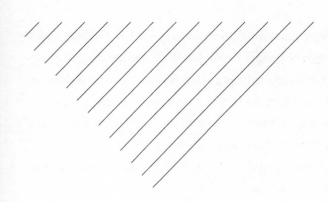

GUBEIKOU SPIRIT

PAN ENTERED GUBEIKOU STATION AT TOP SPEED, HURTLING THROUGH THE CROWDS, HAND ON HER PURSE. It was late and her father would be getting restless, prone to wandering; she needed to get home, get on the train. At the end of the line a guard lazily waved his security wand over her duffel coat, both sides, slowing her down. "I'm in a hurry," she said plaintively.

Down the steps, then, quick-stepping on the too-shallow stairs, dodging the march of people headed in the opposite direction, determinedly clutching their bags as they went. "Let me through!" she cried. But it was 5 p.m. and Gubeikou was crowded. A train had just arrived, disgorging more people now headed to the exits; she was beaten back against the wall by the crowds.

By the time she reached the foot of the stairs the train doors had closed; it had left the station.

That was all right, Pan thought. She'd get the next one. She made her way to a bench, sat down. Haste didn't pay, she reminded herself. Today she'd miscounted the change at the register and ended up 20 yuan short: she'd had to make up the difference. At home as a child, her family had nicknamed her *Ranhou Ne?* because she was always asking "And then?" from the time she was young.

"I got some leeks today," her mother might say.

"And then?"

"I'll make some soup.

"And then?"

"And then we'll eat it."

"And then?"

"And then you'll go to sleep and stop asking questions, baby."

The station filled with people. A middle-aged woman with a perm sat down beside her and fiddled with the clasp on her purse. Opposite them was a yellow ad featuring a grinning Jack Russell terrier jumping in the air to catch what looked like the world, a globe. It was too large: Pan doubted the dog would be able to catch it; it would just bounce harmlessly off his nose.

Another ten minutes passed. Then, an announcement: "The next train will be delayed. We thank you for your understanding."

The train was a marvel, just two years old, state-of-the-art. It had doors that swung open like a singing mouth, emitting a merry chime, and closed after twenty seconds with precision. There were twenty-six lines already built, with another ten under way. No other city in the world had built its subway stations so quickly.

Half an hour passed. The crowd swelled and milled around unhappily, everyone bundled in their coats. Pan was glad she had her seat. Every ten minutes or so, the announcer would return: "The next train will be delayed. We thank you for your understanding."

A pair of teenage boys took off their coats and laid them on the ground and sat atop them. A handful of others followed suit, and then others.

Pan's legs were starting to fall asleep, and she twitched her chilly toes inside her pink boots. It had been a while since anyone else had entered the station, she noticed; they must be turning people away.

Down the platform, a man in a bright-blue coat was the first to try leaving. Indignant, he led a group of half a dozen commuters back up the stairs, where they banged on the access gates, which consisted of tall, solid plates of hammered metal.

One guard must have taken out a stepladder, because suddenly his whole face and part of his torso appeared, peering out over the barriers.

"We'll get the train moving soon," he said kindly. When shouts rang out, he nodded sympathetically. "I know," he said. "You're tired. I'm tired, too. You want to go home and eat a nice meal, rest for a while. I do, too. Please be patient. We'll get there together."

Then he did a little shimmy of his hips, at which the crowd laughed. After the subway system had opened, the government had hired teams of beautiful young women to dress in tight-sheathed skirts and blouses with red sashes across their chests that read TRAIN GODDESSES SERVE THE PEOPLE. During rush hour, they stood on the platform and twitched their hips as they sang the same song:

Thank you for your cooperation, please line up, do not push
Be a civilized passenger, for your safety and that of those around you
We'll get there together.

Pan didn't laugh. Her father was waiting at home, waiting for her to come back and cook dinner. By now he would be pacing anxiously in the living room, where she had left the television on all afternoon in an effort to amuse him, but his favorite program had ended an hour ago and who knew what he might decide to do next: Light the stove? Bang his head repeatedly against a wall?

She took her subway card and waved it over the gates, which flashed a red *X.* "Let us go!" she shouted, but the guard's head had already disappeared.

That night they slept on coats at careful distances from one another, on islands of spread-out newspapers, heads pillowed on bags. The lights never went out. A baby made small keening noises through the night, but did not cry. They were too far down to get any signal, but Pan, who seized a patch of ground near the bathroom at the west end of the tunnel, kept an eye on her phone anyway, watching the time: *11:10, 4:30, 6:32.* Her stomach clenched anxiously any time she thought of her father: perhaps one of the neighbors would have stopped to check on him, she thought to herself. It had happened before.

At 8 a.m. two guards reappeared, this time through a side door marked STAFF ONLY that had been locked overnight. The first came wheeling a cart stacked with boxes of ramen and tall thermoses filled with hot water. Each person got a cup, a toothbrush, and a sliver of soap, which came in pouches that bore the stamped white letters HUMANITARIAN SUPPLIES.

"Repairs still under way," he said shortly.

A man dressed in an untidy, reflective smock, the kind that street cleaners wore, got up, brushing himself off. "You can't treat us like this!" he shouted. "We have things to do. Let us go."

The first guard shook his head regretfully. "Passengers must exit at a different station from where they entered," he said. "It's in the rule book."

The second guard taped a sheet of paper to the wall. *Owing to a mechanical breakdown,* it ran in printed letters, *trains at Gubeikou Station will be delayed. We assure passengers they will get to their destinations. Thank you for your cooperation.* A red seal was affixed in one corner.

"Let us out with you," another man said, pointing at the door through which they'd entered; a third guard was wheeling in another cart.

"Can't do that," the first guard said. He tapped the STAFF ONLY sign and began to lay out trays of plastic utensils, washcloths, and napkins. Other passengers gathered, peppering the man with questions: How much longer? What was the problem, exactly? Could their fares be refunded?

"We'll get you to your destination" is all they would reply. They would take messages to loved ones, they said. They would ensure work units were notified.

One of the teenage boys darted toward the door. In response, the second guard unsheathed an electric baton and whirled it about his person once, striking the young man, who dropped to the ground and began quietly moaning.

"Look what you made me do," the guard said angrily.

In a matter of minutes the men had erected a small supply station near one end of the platform, complete with soy milk, crackers, instant noodles, coloring books, pencils, and stacks of coarse yellow blankets. "Thank you for your cooperation," they said to the crowd, before leaving. "We'll get you moving soon."

That day, the two teenage boys tried scaling the subway turnstiles, but were warned back by guards who stood just outside, faintly visible through the cracks, wielding electric batons. "Down!" they cried, gesturing at signs that said NO CLIMBING.

Pan and others tried standing by the entrance, shrieking repetitively, "Let us out!" There was something both liberating and terrifying in all the fuss they were causing; it made Pan think of her grandmother, who, in her final years, had similarly appeared to lose all inhibitions, shedding her pants in a supermarket, calling neighbors "slovenly" to their faces. It also made Pan's head hurt, and with the guards unmoved, eventually the group's efforts subsided.

By the second day, the train still hadn't come, to everyone's bewilderment. The announcements kept playing: "The next train will be delayed. We thank you for your understanding."

"Soon," the passengers kept telling one another. "It must be soon." Maybe a new part needed ordering. Someone remembered hearing that the trains had been made in Germany. How long did it take to ship something from Germany?

On the third day, the man in the blue coat set off into the tunnels. "We may as well," said the man, named Jun. He tied plastic bags around his shoes; the tunnels were damp, and at night they could hear the sound of water dripping.

"Be careful!" Pan shouted as Jun set off. She liked the slender-hipped way he would stand for hours at the platform, listening earnestly for sounds of the train, the way he helped pick up the scattered ramen lids and neatly stack them after meals. He wasn't from the city; his speech was lilted like that of someone from the country's west.

He returned when they'd nearly given up expecting him, face and hands dirtied. The tunnels extended for miles in all directions, lit by only ghostly lights, he said. He'd gotten lost. The track layout was bewildering, he said. Some tunnels were partly caved in and appeared to have been abandoned halfway, while others led nowhere at all.

The next day he went back in anyway, this time carrying a bag full of their trash, which he used to mark his way. He began disappearing for hours like that, every day. Occasionally the teenage boys would go with him.

"There must be a way out," he said.

Sensing discontent among their charges, the guards wheeled

in a television set, which carried cartoons in the morning, sports games and dramas in the afternoon, and every night, the evening news. There were winter dust storms sweeping the north. There was a new scourge of telephone scams happening; residents were urged to stay on the alert.

Together they slid, uneasily, into this new life. In the mornings, one woman began leading calisthenics sessions to the sound of a tinny transistor radio from one of the guards. The children spent hours chasing one another around the benches on one end of the platform, and did not appear to weary of their game. In the afternoons, adults chatted, watched television, or slept.

At night Pan heard whispered endearments exchanged between a teenage couple who slept a few feet away. Unlike the others, the two seemed utterly content, staying up for hours to eat ramen and watch the television as it flickered in the dark, schoolbags discarded to one side. At times Pan touched the roof of the small cardboard cove she'd erected above her head, offering a semblance of privacy. On its inside, she had stenciled in a number of stars.

She made one for Jun, too, bending and taping the cardboard with care. "You don't have to draw on it," he'd said, and she'd nodded, embarrassed.

One morning, a shout went up in the station: someone had seen a flash of color peeking out from the pile of blankets where one construction worker slept and found that he had been hoarding piles of ramen. When they pulled back his bedding, they found dozens of packets had been stuffed inside.

"Selfish!" shouted the middle-aged woman with a perm. "Don't you think of the rest of us?"

"Get up! Apologize!"

Eventually the group took a vote, and a retired professor among them was chosen to manage the ramen. A sign was drawn up and pasted to the supply station: NO SEEKING PERSONAL BENEFITS: TAKE ONLY WHAT YOU NEED. Later that afternoon (some had begun to eye the professor with suspicion), a second vote was taken and it was decided that they would instead draw up ramen ration tickets, to be handed out every day, and that system lasted for a few days before the guards brought in additional boxes and there was an excess of ramen anyway and everyone abandoned it.

Pan thought of the first time she'd taken a train, thirteen years ago with her mother, before she'd passed away from stomach cancer. Her father had been there, too; it was before his accident, before his confusion had set in, before his illness had turned him into an invalid. She had been ten, and they had been going to see the famous karst landscapes of the south. The train was a hulking green locomotive that carried them for hours, and when they arrived, the air was hot and humid and the hills lush with foliage. Later she would understand her mother was already sick at the time, and this was a final trip for them all to help say goodbye.

Time passed. At night, the baby cried. Jun ventured into the tunnels less frequently, and, like the others, started sleeping for long intervals during the day. "When will the train come?" they asked the guards every morning. "Together we'll get there," they replied, like manic pharmacists given only one pill to administer. The calisthenics woman stopped leading group exercises in the morning after she came down with a cold; dampness from the tunnel had caused it, she was sure.

And then in the middle of the afternoon, two weeks on, it happened. The air changed abruptly, a wind blew through the station, and a rushing noise grew louder.

"It's a train!" yelled one of the children, getting to her feet and dashing near the edge.

"Careful!" her mother warned. "Don't run!"

Others shouted, too. "A train! A train!" Around the floor, several passengers who'd been taking a post-lunch nap fumbled for their glasses and quickly rose to their feet.

Jun was already at the end of the platform, waiting, peering into the tunnel. Pan hurried to join him. "Do you see it?"

"I see it."

The light was getting stronger, streaming through the thick air of the tunnel. The crowd lined up around them, watching. The light grew nearer; there was a honking sound. The train entered the station, moving fast. Inside they could see the train car was empty. There was a moment, too late, when everyone realized that it was not going to slow. It did not stop.

After it departed the station, they sat around dazedly, trying to console one another. "Next time," they said. "It's a good sign, anyway."

A short while later, the sound of the Train Goddesses' song came on the audio system.

Thank you for your cooperation, please line up, do not push
Be a civilized passenger, for your safety and that of those around you
We'll get there —

Then it was abruptly cut off, as though an order had been quickly countermanded.

Later, lying in bed, it occurred to Pan that the careful trails of debris that Jun had been leaving had probably been obliterated by the train. It didn't matter, she told herself. So far his periodic searches hadn't yielded anything, anyway. She suspected he was keeping them up just as a way to be alone: twice she'd seen him shrug off the teenage boys who tried to join him.

Days drew themselves out, days in which Pan, like the others, spent hours prone in bed. After long days on her feet at work, and long nights caring for her father, for the first time in years, she found she could sleep for twelve, thirteen hours straight: such richness, such intoxication. At times it was an effort to pull herself out of bed, to push herself to think of what was required of her now.

"Something's wrong," Pan told the group one morning nearly a month after they were stranded, slowly stirring her ramen. "We're never going to get out. Not unless we do something."

"It's a mechanical issue," said one man who worked in a metallurgical plant and snored loudly through the night. "Have a little patience."

"Patience?" Jun said. "It's been weeks."

"What do you have to do outside that's so important, anyway?" the woman with the perm said. Her voice sounded coquettish, and Jun's face flushed. It was true that he didn't have a wife or children waiting for him, like some of the passengers did. It was true that he would not be missed at the factory, either; they would just move another man up the line.

"Anyway, it's not so bad in here," a woman who worked as a schoolteacher said, sensing his discomfort. "They're taking good care of us."

Since the first days, the guards had brought in mattresses, folding tables, chairs, and pillows. They'd wheeled in extra television sets and for meals had begun serving simple boxed lunches: steamed buns, sandwiches, fried noodles. There were towels, even a badminton set, lots of paper and markers and pens for the children, a few boxes of books and videos. What else did they need?

"That's not the point," Pan said.

"What is the point?" the retired professor said, with what sounded like genuine curiosity, as though she were a student who'd posed an interesting academic question.

Pan stared at him crossly, not knowing what to say.

"I'm getting more rest than I have in years," said a man to her right, and a few of those assembled laughed, as if he'd been joking.

"So you aren't upset?" Pan said, appealing to the group.

"Of course we're upset," the professor said. "But it doesn't do any good to be anxious. Just calm down."

"I am calm!" Pan said. Then she turned away and walked back to her blankets, slowly and deliberately, to show how calm she was, and to camouflage the heat around her eyes.

It took two days to hatch her plan, and then one night after everyone had gone to sleep, she arranged her three other co-conspirators by the staff door. Jun was the one who'd had the good idea to lay additional blankets on the floor and recline on them, as though they'd simply chosen to move their sleeping spots. "There are cameras," he said. "They could be watching."

The next morning, the four of them woke early and listened intently for sounds of movement, each holding an extra blanket. When the door's lock turned and the first guard entered, Jun sprang up and flung a blanket over him. It was harder than they'd expected: one of the teenage boys had to rush to Jun's aid before the two of them managed to pinion the guard's arms to his side.

By then the second guard had entered, baton aloft, but also disappeared sputtering into a blanket. Farther down the platform, heads were beginning to turn.

"Hurry!" Pan yelled to the other passengers, as she and the second teenage boy fought to keep the blanket pulled tight and the guard's arms pinned to his side and to wrestle him to the ground. "Someone get the door!"

"Help!" the boys cried. "Help!"

No one moved. In another moment, roused by the commotion, half a dozen other guards had rushed in, pulling the blankets from their colleagues' heads and administering shocks to Jun and the two teenage boys. Pan they left alone: she registered the surprise on their faces, seeing she was female. "Wait!" she screamed. "Please!" They ignored her and gave Jun and the other boys a few halfhearted kicks as they left, bloodying Jun's nose, taking their still-laden cart with them.

After that another vote was taken: Pan and Jun and the teenage boys weren't allowed anywhere near the staff door in the mornings.

"You'll get us into trouble," the woman with the perm scolded them. "Don't you realize, we depend on them for everything?"

"We could have escaped, if more of you had just helped," Jun said angrily, rubbing his head, still sore from being struck by the baton.

"Yes, and what would we have done once we got there?" said a man with a small, pointed face and a shadow of a mustache, who monopolized the bathroom in the morning. "Do you think we wouldn't have been punished?"

"We just wanted to get out," Pan pleaded. "We have important things to do outside."

"Are you saying the rest of us don't have important things to do outside?" the woman with the perm said indignantly.

"It's not the guards' fault," the construction worker said abruptly, and everyone turned to him in surprise. It was rare for him to comment at all.

That night, without saying anything to anyone, Pan defiantly pulled her mattress across the platform, close to Jun's. In the middle of the night, after she'd gotten up to use the bathroom, she came back and lay down, tensing, wondering if he was awake. After a few minutes, she stretched out her arm and let her hand rest on top of his blankets, where it stayed for perhaps thirty seconds, until he grabbed it and pulled it inside. She let out a low laugh and rolled toward him.

Two months after they were stranded, the country's state broadcaster sent a team to do a report on the group, dispatching reporters to film their badminton games and to interview the passengers. The guards let them respectfully through as the stationmaster, a woman they'd never seen before, wearing a shiny badge and a black tricornered hat, supervised.

The reporters moved through the crowd, picking their subjects. "Sometimes I despair, but I trust in the authorities," the middle-aged woman with a perm said, lip trembling, in the clip that all the news stations aired that evening. "Together we'll get this train moving!"

Back in the studio, the broadcaster nodded and intoned to the camera, "The spirit of Gubeikou Station is strong."

The next day, theirs was a front-page item, under the headline GUBEIKOU SPIRIT. The newspapers carried each of their names, in a double-page spread, along with their photos, opposite an editorial that praised them for their bravery, for "inspiring a nation with their fortitude and optimism."

The atmosphere in the tunnel changed as they pored over the papers the guards had brought that morning, examining their photos. The woman with the perm asked for, and was promised, extra copies.

After breakfast, the retired professor called a meeting. "It's time we organized ourselves," he said. "We have been here two months, and we may be here much longer. The nation is watching us," he said sententiously. "We need to be role models."

Pan made a face and turned to Jun, waiting to see his expression, but to her surprise his eyes were trained on the professor's face, and he was nodding.

"Look at this trash," the professor said, gesturing at the detritus around the tables where they'd eaten. "The bathrooms are a mess, too. We need to organize cleanup crews. We need discipline. We need a schedule."

There was a sound of general assent. "We represent the Gubeikou Spirit!" he said. "We need to come together."

Soon the group had drawn up a list of tasks. Jun volunteered to lead the cleanup crews. The woman with the perm said she'd help run morning calisthenics. The schoolteacher said she'd tutor the children, and asked for volunteers to help. Another woman offered to lead a team to do regular laundry: two items per person per week. They would use the bathroom sinks. The construction worker said he would hang some clotheslines.

A sudden camaraderie seemed to have seized the group. Looking around, Pan felt her skepticism weaken. "I'll help work with the children on their sums," she offered, and felt herself embraced by a smile from the teacher.

The woman with the perm began singing a chorus from the Train Goddesses' song, giggling, shuffling her hips. A little self-consciously, as though they were on camera, the rest of the crowd caught the tune, too:

Thank you for your cooperation, please line up, do not push
Be a civilized passenger, for your safety and that of those around you
We'll get there together.

After that news broadcast, donations started to flood into the station. First it was pallets of dehydrated beef sticks and tins of cookies. Then a store donated piles of new down jackets. One culinary school down the street offered to have its trainees cook for them, and fresh, hot meals began arriving twice a day. To the group's delight, someone sent an old karaoke machine as well, and soon the afternoons were punctuated by the sound of people warbling lustily, taking turns at the microphone.

The guards, too, turned unexpectedly solicitous. After seeing TV commercials for a new kind of fried chicken, the guards brought them samples. When the retired professor complained he was chilly, they sent in an electric heater. When the group wearied of their existing stock of videos, more arrived.

"It's better here than on the outside," a few of the stranded passengers were heard to joke, and others agreed.

Every now and then, the announcements still sounded— "The next train will be delayed. We thank you for your understanding" —but at longer intervals now, and someone had turned the volume down. It was possible, at times, to forget that they were even in a train station. After the news broadcast, more reporters kept arriving, and with them new comforts, as well. The stationmaster ordered couches and more television sets. There was a new program featuring the palace intrigue and romances of a family with two daughters unlucky in love that the group assembled daily to watch, shouting and jeering at one sister, cheering the other on, Pan's head curled on Jun's shoulder.

And meanwhile, the train system kept growing. In the distance, if they craned their necks just right, they could sometimes hear the sound of hammering and drilling. There were twenty-eight lines now open throughout the city, the newscasters said. By the end of the year, there'd be twenty-nine. "With the Gubeikou Spirit," an anchor said one night, "we will continue to persevere, to build the world's most advanced train system!"

At that, the crowd on the platform cheered. They were more considerate of one another, stood a little more upright. The mayor had come to see them, had shaken their hands and posed for a photo before a red banner that bore the words GUBEIKOU SPIRIT. In the mornings, after calisthenics, they ran twenty laps around the platform together, laughing as they tried to round the corners without knocking into one another. In the afternoons, they traded off taking care of the baby, who had grown a soft cloud of hair and begun issuing her sunshiny smile to anyone who looked at her.

To her surprise, Pan found she liked working with the children, helping them with their math, joining them as they colored. On large sheets of paper, she encouraged them to create jungle scenes and geometric patterns, big whorls of colors and diamonds that they taped to the subway walls.

It was only late at night that her thoughts turned, reluctantly, to her father. By now, surely the neighborhood committee had taken charge of his care, she told herself. Perhaps he didn't miss her, she thought—some days he was so confused. She was a poor caretaker, she thought guiltily, working long hours, always away: he might do better in a real institution.

Still, lying near Jun, she found herself restlessly trying to conjure up new methods of escape anyway. They could revolt en masse and climb over the turnstiles—surely some of them would get away. They could refuse food, refuse water.

The next morning, Jun would gently dissuade her. "At this point, we just need to be patient," he said. "We've done all we can. If you haven't noticed," he added, "most people here are actually pretty happy."

He got up and went to play badminton; in recent weeks he'd begun a heated competition with the construction worker. Disgustedly, Pan ate two extra bowls of ramen for lack of anything else to do, and then stopped. Across the way, the calisthenics woman had started up the karaoke machine and was beginning a bouncy rendition of a folk tune with two other women. Pan lay down, shut her eyes, and again fell into a deep slumber.

One morning, the guards came in and affixed a new circular to the walls. *Attention,* it ran. *Gubeikou Station is currently conducting track work. Passengers are advised to stay off the tracks until further notice.*

A ripple of interest ran briefly through the group, then dissipated. The woman with the perm was diligently leading an aerobics session, which was running behind because a few people had slept late, and the group was anxious to finish and have their breakfast (fried mushrooms and steamed rice porridge with pickled vegetables, which smelled very good indeed). It was an unnecessary notice, anyway: Jun and the teenage boys had long ago given up their quest to find a way out through the tunnels.

Shortly after the notice went up, another train arrived. Everyone paused what they were doing and looked up as a rushing sound grew nearer, and a horn sounded full blast. Some of the children moved toward the platform, but the adults simply froze and watched. The locomotive, when it entered, was full of people, they saw: a pack of dusty-faced commuters looking tired and sallow under the fluorescent lights. It zoomed forward without slackening its speed, and, in another moment, it was gone.

Afterward, the adults went back to quietly chatting, struck by seeing so many strangers after so many months. "That was strange," the professor said aloud, as though to himself.

"They looked so unhappy," someone said.

"It's not easy, being outside," the calisthenics woman said, nodding.

Someone turned on the television: the evening newscast was starting up again. Jun and two women on duty moved around and began collecting plates and stacking them on platters for the guards to remove the next day.

That night the newscast was about the job losses being suffered at two steel refineries that were shutting down. For several weeks, the news had all been in a similar vein, a steady drumbeat; the economy was slowing. There was a crime spree in certain neighborhoods; news anchors advised viewers to lock their doors. "Sad," the construction worker said with a sigh, and the others agreed.

After that, trains started coming into the station every day or two. Sometimes they arrived with horns blaring, other times they silently sped through, all their lights off. Twice they saw that the cars had people inside: once, another group of commuters, and another time, a man in an orange repair suit who stood alone, tinkering with a light.

Each time the train never slowed, never stopped. While most of them learned to ignore the trains' appearances, their repeated arrivals seemed to drive one woman, with a spotted face and a badly knitted sweater, over the edge. After each one departed, she would sit in a corner rocking back and forth by herself, muttering. When the next train arrived, she would chase it and pound her arms against the swift-moving body of the locomotive, terrifying those around her, who eventually began forcibly restraining her whenever one arrived. "She could hurt herself like that," they said to one another. "She could fall onto the tracks." But the trains came at all hours of day and night, and it wasn't possible to watch her. Eventually they asked the guards for a short length of chain with which to tether her to a drainpipe by the bathroom.

They moved her mattress and placed a television set in front of her. "It's for your own good," they told her. "We don't want you to get hurt." The woman howled at first, but eventually quieted.

The woman reminded Pan of her father. In the afternoon, she would sit and draw pictures by her side as the woman watched, fascinated. She began bringing her plates of food during meals, to make sure she ate properly.

"More celery," she'd say, imitating herself when she was with her father. "Eat some fruit." The woman would make an assortment of pleased-sounding noises at Pan's attentions. It could not be determined if she had always been so incoherent, or if it was life at Gubeikou that had made her so.

When the trains came, the woman would rise up and lunge at them, as though the locomotive had wronged her family in a past lifetime, her chain rattling. The other passengers speculated about her in hushed tones: Where had she been going the day they'd been stranded, anyway? What would happen to her when they were freed?

"Poor thing, no work unit would want her. She's lucky she wound up here."

The professor had the bright idea of finding the long-ago newspaper article that had listed all those stranded. Together, they located her picture wonderingly: it said she was an accountant.

A chorus of indignation broke out. "Not possible—look at her," the professor said.

"It must be an error," the others said.

Then one day, the train snuck up on them. It was late in the evening. The kids were playing down at one end of the platform, by the badminton net. They had just finished eating their dinner, roast pork and steamed rice and braised bamboo shoots, and now that the plates had been stacked and put aside, most of the group was congregated around the television, watching a detective show. Pan was leaning back in her chair, her legs casually slung over Jun's lap, comfortably encased in one of the newly donated sweatshirts the guards had unpacked the other day, which read GUBEIKOU SPIRIT across the front. It was a Friday, but it might as well have been a Tuesday or a Wednesday; it made no difference—all the days ran together. The atmosphere was warm and convivial: the retired professor was already nodding off in his chair, and around the table, some of the others smiled at the sight.

The volume on the television was turned up, and it was only the sound of metal rasping against metal that made them look up. Across the way, a beam of light was streaming through the tunnel: another train was coming through. Down the platform, the woman was on her feet, yanking futilely at her chain and lunging forward, her chain clanging noisily against the pipe. The group frowned. "Calm down!" the middle-aged woman with the perm shouted.

The rushing sound of the train was quieter than usual, though, and in another moment the group realized why. The train wasn't moving that quickly; in fact, it was slowing down. It had stopped.

In another moment the train's doors had opened with a merry chime. The train car was empty. Its insides had a faintly yellow cast, the carpet dirty and worn.

"It's stopped!" someone cried. Pan stood and gazed at the open doors, heart pounding, joy and fear coursing through her veins in equal measure.

The group was silent. On the screen, a detective was rushing down a set of stairs in pursuit of a woman in flight. Pan turned toward her sleeping pallet to grab a few possessions. No, there wasn't time. "Jun!" she called. "It's here!"

He was still seated, slowly tying his laces, not looking at her. "It might not be safe," the professor warned. No one moved.

"We should ask first," one of the others muttered. "Find out what's going on."

"This could be our only chance!" cried Pan. A few wary pairs of eyes glanced over from the television. "Come *on*, get up! What have we been waiting for?"

The train's warning chime sounded: in another moment, the doors would close. "Hurry!" she yelled, but the others stayed seated. Incredulous, she wrenched her eyes from the group and hurtled toward the train, socked feet flashing white. Farther down the platform, she heard the sound of the woman's metal chain rasping and felt a twinge of guilt, but kept running. Two of the teenage boys rose and joined her. The doors slid shut. "Pan, wait!" Jun shouted.

She didn't hear him. She stood panting, exhilarated and afraid. She was already through the door.

ACKNOWLEDGMENTS

Thank you to all the people who opened their hearts to this manuscript and worked tirelessly to deliver it into the world, especially to Rayhané Sanders, for her sharp insights and early belief in these stories, to Naomi Gibbs, for her graceful edit, and to the rest of the wonderful Houghton Mifflin Harcourt team, including Taryn Roeder, Lori Glazer, Michael Dudding, Mark Robinson, Laura Brady, Millicent Bennett, and Jenny Xu, as well as Michael Taeckens, Jade Wong-Baxter and Amy Edelman, Chris White and the team at Scribner UK, and all of Massie & McQuilkin's coagents. I am deeply indebted to you for your help and many kindnesses.

ACKNOWLEDGMENTS

Thank you to the Fulbright program and the *Wall Street Journal* for the chance to live in so many places that fired my imagination, and thank you to the friends and colleagues who made those years so special. Thanks in particular to Tom Pellman for his thoughtful comments on these stories, and to Kate Lloyd for her surefooted advice throughout.

To my parents, thank you for teaching me the importance of words, for countless childhood trips to the library and for showing me what love and hard work look like. You gave me my first home and opened the door to so many more through books. For that, and more, I'm very grateful.

Above all, I owe my greatest thanks to Ben, who read each story as it was written and encouraged me to keep going: without you, these stories wouldn't exist, and would be immeasurably poorer. I still can't believe I get to share my life with someone so brilliant, funny, and kind; every day with you and JK is a gift and an adventure. I love you so much. Thank you.